D1131819

THE EXECUTIONER

THE
EXECUTIONER

by Pierre Boulle

author of
"The Bridge Over the River Kwai," etc.

THE VANGUARD PRESS
NEW YORK

THE EXECUTIONER

1

O N E

I was sitting in a restaurant in the magical city of Yin-Yang. Before me stood a bowl of rice and three plates laden with exotic delicacies. A Chinese book lay open by my left hand. I would decipher a column of characters, then try to fish out a morsel of food with my chopsticks, both these operations presenting equal difficulties. After a lengthy tussle I shut the book and concentrated all my attention on the meal.

"There's not a single interesting suggestion in this novel," I said to myself peevishly. "It's the crime of a madman. I won't get anything out of it."

It was an utterly incoherent detective story. I realized with some embarrassment that I had spoken out loud. The old Chinese sitting opposite was looking across at me with an amused expression on his face. His chopsticks were poised in mid-air and, branching out from his fist, seemed to trace a "V for Victory" sign above the table.

"Sir," he said in French, and in a sententious tone of voice, "there are some things that can't be learned from books."

"I know," I replied pensively. "There are many things that can't be learned from books: literature, for instance."

"Sir," he went on, "I gather you're intrigued by reprehensible acts. I heard you say something about a crime committed by a madman. Offenses of that sort can sometimes be extremely interesting. I was involved in one myself."

I felt a thrill of excitement and examined the old gentleman with relish.

First of all I must tell you I am a professional writer and that in my work I employ certain methods that are not universally approved.

My first rule is never to be spontaneous in my stories; never to yield to the demands of my mind (such weakness, to my way of thinking, is pardonable only in extreme youth) and thereby contribute to the hideous sin in which guilty old men recklessly encourage the writers of my generation. My second rule is never to observe what is going on around me. Thus my stories are neither the outcome of an inward urge, scorned out of modesty as a vulgar source of inspiration, nor an overclose examination of humanity, condemned as a crude indiscretion. I never write the truth.

My chief concern is to distinguish myself from others. With this aim in view, my particular plan consists in imagining a priori a peculiar situation that, by human standards, is utterly improbable. Above all, I do my best to achieve an effect of surprise; and when several possibilities of this sort come up for consideration, I naturally choose the one that presents the most outrageous and most inconceivable absurdity.

Then, taking into account that my readers, after all, are human beings, I strive to endow the situation with a deceptive appearance of rationality and to bring it to life by means of a false logical sequence that perfidiously tends to make it acceptable. I thus achieve a further factitious effect: the effect of contrast.

As you might imagine, the stumbling block that constantly confronts me in this systematic composition is the main character. I have not succeeded in eliminating the obstacle entirely, and it almost always demands a model that one is apt to look for in real life. But how am I to take my characters from real life when I endow them with absurd reasoning? How am I to choose them from among us, since they have to behave in every circumstance like puppets?

I have gotten around this difficulty by drawing on the Chinese, an utterly unreal people—though very much alive—from a different world who can supply the patient forger of facts with sufficiently extravagant subjects by the thousand.

This is simply to account for my presence after dark in the magical city of Yin-Yang. I feel so much more at home in a Chinese atmosphere. Sometimes, as on this occasion, I also venture into one of those improbable restaurants where the smell of rotten eggs mingles with the scent of spices, in the hope that a look at the surrealist characters to be found there will put me in a suitable frame of mind for the creation of those weird adventures that are my daily bread and provide me with an artificial compensation for my total lack of sensibility.

But on this particular evening I was feeling uneasy and tortured by remorse. For several months, true to my word, I had not set foot in the city of Yin-Yang. Only the day before, after a paternal word of warning from my guardian angel, I had sworn never to enter its gates again.

My guardian angel always keeps a close watch over me. He is deeply hurt when I reject the models he favors, and my escapades had alarmed him. He kept telling me over and over again:

"Beware, oh beware, of the twisting alleys and deadly lanes that make a treacherous spider's web of this city, a hazard for inexperienced souls. Put an end, I beseech you, to this pursuit of Chinese shadows.

"Paint men as they are, I implore you, and not as they have no business to be. Art has nothing to do with research. You frighten me when I see you toiling away among those dragons. Stop making such an effort. Let your heart overflow. There's nothing to be said for the weird and outlandish. Don't expect *chinoiseries* to be accepted as a literary form.

"The writer's art consists in reproducing familiar clichés, then embellishing them and embellishing them again, and finally setting them in a delicately chiseled framework. His talent is judged by the credibility of his characters, that is to say, by the normality of their thoughts and actions. I anticipate your objection: you're going to tell me that the Chinese do exist. That's a poor excuse. Don't imagine that a living creature is necessarily plausible. He must also have no unusual feature, no original quality, no peculiarity, and must also have been conceived like this by several generations of your predecessors and introduced by them in hundreds of works I can refer to, before I can accept his plausibility. I know thousands of men and women like this on whom you could base a story, and your choice would be made still easier by the fact that in the long run they boil down to a mere three or four. I laugh and grieve at the same time when I look at your vain endeavors to discover new characters and see you finally return from your quest with a synthetic monster in whom it is all the more difficult to believe in so far as his grimaces are vaguely, grotesquely reminiscent of certain human expressions. How can you hope to be convincing with Chinese as your models?

"If you don't follow my advice people will begin to think you're nothing but a humbug, and that would mortify me."

Naturally, I was not in the least inclined to adopt these principles, but I have a high regard for my guardian angel's wisdom, experience, and solicitude. One of us was right. Since he has progressed beyond the age of doubt and reached that of mathematical certainty, he is convinced he's the one and not I. He had almost succeeded in convincing me as well. The grief I was causing him filled me with confusion, and that is why I had for several months resisted the attraction that the city of Yin-Yang exercises over me— a noteworthy feat, for this attraction is as strong as the lure of forbidden pleasures.

And this evening I had yielded to its spell. This evening I had not only filled my lungs with the noxious fumes that poison its atmosphere but I had entered a temple of extravagance where people eat with little sticks. This evening, as in the days of my most shameful excesses, I had supplemented these pernicious stimulants with an example of reading matter that has inspired me with the most grotesque plots: a Chinese detective novel.

I had given myself the excuse that I was taking no risks since I was on my guard. My escapade would have no consequences. I would speak to no one. I would accept no suggestion without first subjecting it to the test of common sense. I had even cast my book aside with scorn as soon as I thought I detected a devilish whiff of fantasy in it that insulted my Cartesian nostrils.

And here, on his own initiative, was an old Chinese engaging me in conversation! Here he was, talking about a crime: a crime committed by a madman, and presenting a certain amount of interest! I thought— I swear I did—of my guardian angel. I bit my tongue and maintained a heroic silence. But he persisted.

"As I was saying, sir, I was once involved in a criminal affair whose hero cannot be regarded as a man of sound mind. Yet I was wrong to call him a madman. He wasn't mad, and experts eventually decided he was completely responsible for his behavior. It was a strange case."

"A strange case," I murmured involuntarily.

"Strange and at the same time simple, sir," he said.

I have said enough to indicate that the adjective "strange" exercises an unusual fascination over me. But when it is accompanied by the epithet "simple" my mind is seized by an absolute frenzy. In fact, these two qualities, strangeness and simplicity, are more or less my only artistic criteria; the first, for the reasons of the effect to be produced that I've already explained; the second, for less base motives, which I have not yet been able to elucidate. On two or three occasions only have I encountered the coincidence of these virtues difficult to reconcile but not contradictory, and in each of these miraculous circumstances I have felt exalted to a superhuman pitch, infinitely closer to Olympus than to this sorrowful vale of tears.

13

Once it was over a face . . . but I have sworn never to yield to an inward urge.

My good resolutions for the evening suddenly appeared somewhat exaggerated. After all, I said to myself in order to allay a faint misgiving, I can listen to him with one ear and still be free to forget whatever he has to say. One step more, and I had made up my mind not to let him escape until he had told me his story, even if I had to resort to force.

But first I decided to rely on diplomacy. I knew it was bad form, with men of his race, to betray too much curiosity. I pretended in a Machiavellian way not to show any more than a polite interest in his words.

"Really?" I murmured.

"Most truly, sir," he replied.

After that I commended him on his advanced age. I know how to deal with the Chinese.

"Venerable sir," I said, "I'm a mere stripling, but I should like to benefit from your experience, which, I feel sure, must be considerable."

"You're right, sir," he agreed. "My experience is considerable."

Then I asked him if he would do me the honor of sharing a flagon of *choum,* or rice wine, with me, and I declared myself ready to listen humbly to his reminiscences if he saw fit to acquaint me with them.

A furtive gleam came into his eye, then he heaved a deep sigh.

"It would be a pleasure, sir, for there are moments

14

in a man's life when he feels the need to imbibe a little alcohol."

"I like that phrase," I said. "There are moments in a man's life—"

"—when he feels the need to imbibe a little alcohol. That's a Confucian maxim."

"This evening, I feel one of those fleeting moments has arrived."

"So do I; but I've already finished my meal, and custom forbids the absorption of alcohol at this stage."

"Then let us start another meal, venerable sir," I suggested.

He thought the matter over and seemed to appreciate the quality of this compromise. A waiter cleared the table and came back with a multitude of plates containing little bits and pieces of the diverse animal life that inhabits the forests, seas, and skies of China. The bottle of *choum* was placed between us. Then the old man embarked on his story.

T W O

"Sir," he began, "this adventure occurred in the province of Li-Kang, where I was born and where I spent part of my life. The province of Li-Kang lies embedded between India, Tibet, Burma, and the rest of China. The climate there is harsh, communications difficult, industry poorly developed, large towns scarce. For all this we are not savages. We abide by the traditions of the ancient and precious Chinese civilization. We have adopted certain Tibetan rites whose picturesque quality beguiled our forefathers, and, in spite of our proverbial xenophobia, we have accepted certain Western practices, brought back no doubt from India by our travelers, that seemed likely to enrich our ceremonies.

"Respect for one's elders is observed by us as much as the cult of one's ancestors. Wise men, men of letters, are held in high esteem. That at least was the characteristic of my province when I was living in Yi-Ping, and there is no reason to believe that the customs have since changed."

"Yi-Ping?"

"That's the main town, the seat of the provincial government, the town where I once humbly but honorably exercised the profession of physician. But let me specify the degree of our civilization, for too many foreigners, among those who have not traveled, regard us as barbarians."

I told him I had traveled and that my views were different. But he insisted on describing in detail the various institutions of his province. He laid particular emphasis on its legislation. He dwelt at great length on the perfection of the Chinese legal code and the wisdom of the mandarins responsible for administering justice. I listened to him with half an ear, impatient to hear him embark on his story. He finally did so when I declared that I could see no difference between the laws of Li-Kang and those of the most highly developed countries in the world.

"Well, I used to exercise my profession in the town of Yi-Ping and, as my digression may have led you to suspect, I was frequently called in to collaborate with the tribunals in the capacity of a medical expert. I appreciated this honor, but among the delicate tasks

17

that made me a modest auxiliary of Justice there was one which afforded me no joy. In fact, it was an ordeal, and it was only because of a sense of duty that I could bring myself to accomplish it. This reluctance was inexcusable, but perhaps you will make allowances when I tell you that I was required to attend all the capital executions in Yi-Ping and to officiate from the medical point of view."

"I absolve you, venerable sir," I said. "I can see only too clearly why you should have regarded that task as an ordeal."

"I am deeply thankful. . . . Well, sir, I shall now invite you to one of those grim performances—namely, the one that took place at the beginning of the year nineteen hundred and twenty-one, according to your calendar. I shall try to re-enact it for your benefit as faithfully as my memory permits."

At these words I trembled as I thought of my guardian angel. I sighed. I knit my brows and, assuming my most solemn tone, said firmly:

"It's impossible for me to follow you on that course, venerable sir. You're trying to drag me off and lead me down the paths of temptation. And I'm a little sorry about it, because you had whetted my appetite, but from now on all such fantasies are forbidden me. In no circumstances will I listen to the description of an execution, even though it did take place in China over thirty years ago, and actually in the province of Li-Kang, for whose civilization I have a high regard. I see what you're up to. You're trying to achieve an effect of horror. It's a trick, and the most contemptible trick of all. Never speak to me again. Vanish from my sight. I'll find some other source of inspiration."

But the old Chinese did not vanish.

On the contrary, he made himself more massive and substantial than ever, and one of his chopsticks pointed at me like a peremptory index finger.

"I'm not striving after 'effects,' sir. I'm telling you a story because you very politely asked me to do so, and because it gives me pleasure. If you find it unbearable, you are at liberty to block your ears, to think of something else and forget me, as a reader forgets a book that bores him. As for vanishing, I find your request presumptuous, since you are here in China, in the town of Yin-Yang."

"Forgive me, venerable sir," I said. "I had no wish to offend you. Your story doesn't bore me in the least. But couldn't you eliminate such cruel and repellent scenes as an execution?"

"I must make my story intelligible, and that episode is indispensable. Besides, who mentioned cruelty? I can see you have lent an ear to those legends that represent the Chinese as inhuman creatures who delight in certain refined forms of torture. You ought to know that, though the death penalty is applied in the province of Li-Kang, the stake and other punishments were abolished ages ago. Our condemned men are dispatched with a minimum of suffering: by decapitation. We don't employ a perfected machine, as you do, but the balance and temper of the sword,

19

and the strength and skill of the executioner are such that the operation is almost always performed in a single stroke.

"You ought to know, furthermore, that the death sentence is pronounced by our tribunals only for particularly serious offenses and that, since the governor indulges freely in his right to reprieve, necks actually are very rarely severed in the province of Li-Kang— there were no more than half a dozen executions in Yi-Ping during the three years previous to the date when my story begins."

"Let's not talk about cruelty," I said. "I was wrong. On the contrary, I defer to such moderation. I maintain, however, that the grisly details inevitably associated with such scenes, however humanized they may be, cannot appear in any of my stories."

"Then, since that is your wish, sir, I shan't say a word."

"I spoke a little hastily, venerable sir," I hurriedly assured him. "Are you quite sure your story is really strange?"

"Strange and simple, as I told you before. But you will never hear it, for your nerves are too delicate."

"Devil!" I exclaimed. "Tempter!—I mean, venerable sir! Will you at least guarantee that this execution is a logical outcome of your story?"

"I guarantee it, sir, and I am deeply hurt by your suspicions. I fully intended to pass over the more unpleasant details and to concentrate on the essential facts, which can't shock anyone."

"Is that true? Can I trust you implicitly? Are you

certain these facts aren't upsetting?" I said, on the verge of capitulation.

"I give you my word that my story could not offend the sensibilities of a child."

"I wasn't thinking of children, venerable sir," I muttered. "I was thinking of my guardian angel."

"Guardian angels, sir, are unknown in the Chinese world. I abide by the terms of my pledge: the sensibilities of a child."

"Go ahead, then," I said submissively.

THREE

"One morning, sir, I arrived at the central prison of Yi-Ping well before dawn, with orders to attend one of those ceremonies whose description seems to horrify you and, as I said before, had no appeal for me at all.

"In the registry, which was the usual meeting place, I joined the little group of officials who were subjected like myself to this ordeal. The room had been decorated the day before with garlands of brightly colored paper, but was rather dimly illuminated by an oil lamp, the padellas and multicolored lanterns having not yet been lit.

"There were various mandarins there, both great and small, each of them occupying a position in our judiciary administration, which, with a few differences, has its counterpart in yours. I shall call them by the approximate titles that are familiar to you. There was the Mandarin President of the tribunal, the Mandarin Attorney General, the Mandarin Police Chief, and the Mandarin Prison Director, not to mention the condemned man's advocate and myself.

"There were also the representatives of the various religions to which our people subscribe and that offer them a wide choice of godheads, devils, jinns, and dragons. We Chinese are indifferent to religious fervor, but curious in matters of the spirit. Once our imagination is aroused, captivated by the picturesque as much as by tradition, it is always ready to welcome a new fable, provided its heroes are good enough to conform, as they generally do, to our centuries-old principles. Thus we resort to every possible cult when we feel that death is close at hand. That morning, I remember quite clearly, only three were represented—by a Buddhist monk, a Taoist priest, and a sage versed in the rites of Confucius.

"Needless to say, there were also the executioner and his assistants.

"These officials, sir, derived no more pleasure than I from the idea of the part each was to play; in fact, I am certain they all felt slightly sickened. There is no country in the world in which the taking of human life is made an occasion for merriment, and China is no exception. This duty weighed on us heavily.

23

"It was a duty all the same. We had therefore braced ourselves to carry it out with the utmost dignity. We all greeted one another ceremoniously, in the fashion of our country, which is different from yours but perhaps is more appropriate for solemn occasions. It consists in bowing low from the waist, with both hands joined together and held against the breast. To give you a complete picture of the scene, I ought to mention that at the beginning of the year the early hours of dawn are bitterly cold in the province of Li-Kang and we were all dressed in heavy Chinese cloaks with wide sleeves. In spite of this I felt myself shivering."

The Chinese doctor broke off and brooded on this recollection. I was watching him closely and had no difficulty in visualizing the scene he conjured up: a group of Chinese, shivering with cold, muffled up in their long robes, their arms crossed, their hands tucked into their padded sleeves, bowing solemnly to one another in the chilly light of the prison. I shuddered, then drained my glass and begged him to go on with his story.

"After greeting one another, calling the roll, and finding all present, we left the executioner and his assistants in the registry, and in single file, making as little noise as possible in our felt slippers, we made our way to the condemned man's cell, which was situated at the far end of the prison.

"When we arrived, the brass band was already in position, standing silently outside the iron gate.

24

Then, at a signal from the Mandarin President of the tribunal—"

"The brass band?" I exclaimed, unable to believe my ears.

"Isn't that what you call a collection of drums and trumpets? There were also some brass bells from Tibet, and other instruments whose names I don't know in your language but which you would recognize, I think—a sort of hollow wooden mill on the end of a stick, which makes a loud clatter when whirled in the hand."

"Rattles, probably. But what the devil—"

"If certain details are repugnant to you, sir, let me pass over them quickly.

"Well, the Mandarin President of the tribunal gave the signal for reveille to be sounded. The fanfare burst out all at once, with the violence of an explosion, all the instruments sounding at full blast, making the walls of the ancient citadel vibrate. Then the cell door was opened and we went inside. The condemned man was already awake, sir.

"His bedclothes were in a tangle, as though he had spent a disturbed night. His hands were clapped to his ears, which was scarcely surprising, as the din was infernal. His gaze was fixed on the door. His eyes—"

"Please don't describe his eyes," I said, mopping my brow. "I'd sooner hear you talk about the rattles."

"As you like, sir. Well, the rattles stopped, so did the other instruments, and the Mandarin Attorney General went up to the condemned man. He bowed

25

low before him, told him what was in store for him, expressed his regrets, and politely advised him to take courage.

"The condemned man put up a bold front. His limbs were trembling slightly, but he managed to get up and courteously returned the mandarin's greeting. He dressed almost without assistance and was soon ready. We followed him outside. He was flanked by two guards and preceded by the brass band. Our procession filed down the dark corridors of the prison. That slow progress is somewhat grim for the witnesses, sir. It inevitably suggests a funeral procession, for the drums and trumpets play the same tunes in both cases. I never got used to it."

"I can understand your anguish, venerable sir. Put an end to it quickly."

"Eventually we found ourselves back in the registry. In accordance with the ritual, the padellas and paper lanterns attached to the garlands were lit by the assistant executioners. They formed a dazzling vault under which the condemned man was placed. This was the last stage before the scaffold itself, erected in front of the prison, in a courtyard separated from the room by a single heavy door. The musicians had stopped playing and had gone off by a roundabout way to take up their positions outside.

"Now the last formalities had to be observed. By the laws of our country, these are reduced to the minimum that decency requires. Mere respect for the human being demands the observance of a certain ceremonial; however abject the criminal may be, society cannot dispose of him as though of a dangerous beast. So on that morning, as usual, the traditions were scrupulously followed. The joss sticks were lit. The condemned man's signature was registered in several ledgers. He was politely asked what his last wishes might be. He was given permission to write to his family. The priests of the three religions offered him their services, one after another, then all together.

"He refused most of these favors and declared himself ready to die, his only request being to get it over as quickly as possible. I assure you, sir, he was a staunch character. His bearing was exemplary. He had even managed to suppress the tremor that had seized him on waking. I'm not saying this in order to move you to pity, but because it is an important element in my story. He was a vile wretch with several lives on his conscience; but we were grateful to him for not betraying his anguish—always painful for those whose duty it is to assist a man to his end.

"I've no doubt such lamentations must be very trying," I said.

"Sometimes they are literally unbearable. But this time we were spared. The condemned man actually turned down all last-minute privileges, even ignoring the rice cakes offered him.

"All he accepted was the traditional glass of whiskey the prison warden handed him, but this he certainly did accept avidly. The moment he saw it, he was as though hypnotized. He snatched it out of the warden's hand, tore at it so greedily that some of it spilled, and downed it at one gulp like a drunkard. In my opinion, sir, his precipitance was excusable. I think I've already told you there are moments in a man's life when he needs a drink."

My old Chinese doctor paused and, as was apparently his custom every time he enounced this Confucian maxim, he emptied five or six glasses of rice wine in a matter of seconds. Now, with chopsticks clicking like dry bones, he described a long arc with his hand. In the twinkling of an eye he caught up several delicate morsels that he dipped in a black sauce and swallowed down silently.

After having drunk also, I told him I could well understand and excuse the condemned man's behavior. Encouraged, he went on:

"As I say, he drained his glass at one gulp and handed it back with a violent gesture. It was at this point that the executioner, who till then had been lurking in a dark corner, came out of the shadows, throwing off his greatcoat and appearing in the costume fixed by tradition: naked to the waist and dressed solely in a pair of red breeches tightly gathered at the ankles. At the same time, the Mandarin prison warden ordered some firecrackers shot off."

"Firecrackers!"

"Yes, sir, to mark a new phase in the ceremony. Firecrackers and three strokes on a monstrous gong that made us all jump even though we had been expecting them.

"And now it is essential for me to give you a few

more concrete details, to which I beg you to lend your closest attention.

"The executioner stepped into the full light, undeniably presenting an imposing appearance, for this half-naked man with torso ruddy from the cold and breeched in scarlet silk suddenly struck a spectacular note among the dull tones of our dark robes. At that moment, as the gongs and firecrackers hammered away at our eardrums, shattering our nerves, and giving each of us the impression that the prison walls were about to collapse, and as the executioner's assistants, who had already seized the condemned man, proceeded to groom and make him up for the last rites, the condemned man showed signs of agitation for the first time. Despite the tumult, I could hear a low moaning and I fancied his legs were beginning to buckle. Sir, if the assistants had not held him up firmly, he would have pitched forward in a heap."

"I'm not in the least interested in these details," I said. "You promised me—"

"They're an essential part of my story, and that ought to make them acceptable.

"My colleagues and I exchanged an anxious glance. We listened closely but there was no further complaint. I thought—without displeasure, I beg you to believe me—I thought that the condemned man had been seized by a momentary weakness as a result of an overpowering emotion, as frequently happens on these occasions. This was not a novel occurrence in Yi-Ping. At previous executions, I remembered quite

29

clearly, the condemned man had displayed similar faintness just at the very moment, I beg you to note, when the executioner stepped into the dazzling light created by the padellas and lanterns."

"I can't understand why you should make such a point of that, venerable sir"—he had laid a curious emphasis on his last remark—"there's nothing *strange* about it, as you claimed. This behavior seems absolutely normal to me."

"So it does to me, and I'm very happy our opinions should coincide on this point. At the same time, I must underline the self-control the condemned man had shown right up to that moment. The fellow's bearing suggested a physical and moral equilibrium that was capable of withstanding every emotion right up to the final stroke of the sword. He was not the sort of man to fall into a swoon, like a woman with the vapors."

"And yet he fainted away," I observed impatiently. "I'm not at all surprised. I can't understand why you're being so mysterious about it."

"You'll understand later on, I hope. . . . But let me finish the most unpleasant part of the story.

"The assistants completed the ablution. They bound the condemned man hand and foot. They anointed his face with bright colors. The executioner bowed low before him. The henchmen dragged him off. The door swung back on its hinges. Another fanfare blared out. He was lifted onto the scaffold without giving a sign of consciousness.

"I shan't describe in detail the rites that followed.

30

The final episode takes place while the condemned man's head is resting on the block. It consists of traditional kowtows, genuflections, parades, Greek fires and burning incense, accompanied by music played at a faster and faster tempo and with ever-increasing volume until it reaches a sort of climax in which all the instruments, trumpets, drums, bells and rattles break loose in the midst of a display of fireworks and rockets.

"This lasts exactly a quarter of an hour. Then there is a minute of complete silence, and the executioner officiates."

"A quarter of an hour?"

"A quarter of an hour, sir, plus one minute. When the time was up, the executioner performed with his customary skill and competence.

"Then I approached. Hastily—rather too hastily— I examined the body and made out a certificate testifying death by decapitation. I was in a hurry to get it over, I admit."

"I don't blame you," I said.

"You are too kind. Others were less so. When the ceremony ended, and everything had taken place according to the prescribed ritual and we were about to withdraw, something quite extraordinary occurred."

FOUR

"Aha!" I exclaimed. "Something extraordinary?"

"Yes, sir. As the smell of the incense began to fade in the early-morning light. . . ."

"The incense? You're sure it wasn't a whiff of brimstone?"

"I don't know what you mean, sir, but if my story is too crude for you I may as well end it now."

"Traitor! You were saying something quite extraordinary occurred—"

"A blast on a whistle from the Mandarin Chief of Police, who was in the front row of the officials, as I think I told you. This mandarin—a considerable

32

figure: apart from the governor, the most important man in the whole province—had seemed to take a keener and more sustained interest in the execution than he usually did: a suspiciously keen interest. Although he concealed his thoughts behind a mask of politeness, which is a rule with us Chinese at any public gathering, it was undoubtedly distrust that I had detected in his eyes: distrust toward his other colleagues and particularly toward myself. It made an unpleasant impression on me. When the condemned man had moaned and then lost consciousness, the mandarin had approached him with an inquisitive air, shaking his head.

"Well, he gave a blast on his whistle while we were still gathered around the scaffold, and in a moment we found ourselves surrounded by a troop of guards who had been hidden in the corners of the courtyard. Then he asked us not to move and expressed his regret at having to detain us all for a moment or two: just long enough to proceed with his inquiry, interrogate us, and take down our statements on the subject of the crime that had just been committed. He added that he apologized for laying this trap but that his sense of duty required him to catch the culprit, or culprits, red-handed."

"The culprits? Red-handed? I'm afraid I'm all at sea, venerable sir," I said.

"We, too, were all at sea," the Chinese doctor went on after a moment's silence, "and I don't think you could appreciate the extent of our perplexity or the irritating aspect of the dismay that seized us when the chief of police led us into the reception room and posted his guards at the exits. Curious and apprehensive, we asked for some explanation. He hesitated; then, yielding to the pressing request of the two mandarin magistrates, he consented to reveal that it was a case of murder. He had been notified the day before by the governor of the province, who had received a denunciation and had ordered him, he once more explained, to catch the culprit, or culprits, in the very act."

"A case of murder?" I exclaimed with a start.

"A case of murder, sir. Those were his very words."

"And who was the victim?"

"For the time being he wouldn't give us the name of the victim or any other details. He withdrew and left us to ourselves.

"But put yourself in our place, I beseech you. Tell me if, on the face of it, and taking all the circumstances of time and place into account, you might not at least have toyed with the idea that the victim might well be the man whose head had just fallen."

"I'm more and more at sea. Didn't you tell me that the death penalty in the province of Li-Kang was—"

"—provided for and perfectly legal. I can see that at this very moment you're under the same misapprehension that was at the root of our anxiety."

"A misapprehension?"

"A misapprehension, sir. And if you ever write this story, which I can see you are already thinking of doing, I should like to draw your attention to the subtlety of the situation."

"No subtlety," I said firmly. "That's forbidden, and I'm likewise not allowed to demand the slightest intellectual effort on the part of my readers. Let's have a straightforward explanation."

"Well, we were undeniably on duty. We were sure we had followed the prescriptions of the law, but— put yourself in our place, as I said before. Imagine that in the bitter cold of dawn, in the somewhat forbidding atmosphere of a prison, after seeing a head fall as the outcome of a ceremony I have only described to you in part and that is something of an ordeal after all, imagine that you had been requested to hold yourself at the disposal of the courts to answer for a murder, this particular case being a case of *flagrante delicto*. You will then understand perhaps why we, the most honorable men in China, were assailed by a vague misgiving."

"I see you'll never be able to explain yourself more clearly. Pray go on, though. I shall rely on intuition to make up for a lack of logic which surprises me in a man like you."

"One glance at us, sir, would have been sufficient for you to discern the symptoms of that feeling of oppression which I'm finding so hard to describe. The two mandarin magistrates, who in any other circumstance would never have consented to losing face in this way, did not raise the slightest objection. On the contrary, they set a good example of submission

35

to higher authority. They advised us to be patient, pointing out that there was no possible charge against us. They did so in such forceful, persuasive terms that I felt they were trying to convince themselves.

"The Buddhist monk and Taoist priest were both in a deep trance, in accordance with the prescriptions of their respective doctrines. The Confucian sage, finding nothing in his science that could be applied to such a violation of the rites, began to look rather disgruntled. The Mandarin Prison Director had gone white in the face, and I myself was not feeling too easy in my mind. I confess I had to cross my arms firmly across my chest to prevent myself from trembling. Such, sir, can be the effect produced on innocent men under strain by a spectacular deployment of the machinery of justice."

"I'm beginning to see what you mean after all, in spite of your obscurity, and I can well imagine the scene."

"But the executioner's attitude, sir, was the most remarkable of all. I was extremely surprised, because I thought he would have been hardened by his profession and able to control himself in the most trying circumstances. I must describe him to you, for this executioner plays a leading part in my story and he turned out to be a most unusual character.

"While his assistants, who were less affected than the rest of us, philosophically resigned themselves to being under close arrest, he, the executioner, betrayed signs of the utmost agitation. We could hear him talking to himself, muttering unintelligibly, then whimpering under his breath. All of a sudden he appeared to break down. He burst into tears and threw himself at the feet of the mandarin magistrates, beating his breast and crying out:

" 'I'm the one, great mandarins, I'm the one who killed him! I'm the one, I tell you, and I also killed all the others in the last three years!'

"This statement was so ludicrous, sir, and the executioner's emotion so immoderate, that we were all deeply moved. It was an extremely painful sight for us and strained our nerves to the limit. The Mandarin Attorney General, a sensitive little man, began to display a similar lack of self-control and I'm certain I heard him mutter to himself: 'We did it! We did it!'

"The director of the prison likewise lost his composure and our group began to show every sign of the mob hysteria to which the Chinese are sometimes prone in spite of their robust mental constitution.

"A scandal was happily avoided by the Mandarin President of the tribunal. He forced the executioner to rise to his feet, telling him sternly not to behave like a child and reminding him once again that he had only performed his duty, as we all had, which he seemed to have forgotten.

"We were somewhat reassured by the wisdom of these words, but the executioner still seemed to be out of his mind. He kept repeating over and over again, like a maddening refrain: 'I'm the one, I'm the one who killed him, as well as all the others!'

37

"At this stage the Mandarin President decided to put an end to this unseemly exhibition. He ordered two of his assistants to lay hold of him and keep him quiet. The executioner offered no resistance. After a while he calmed down and lapsed into a state of deep gloom.

"We were kept there, locked up and under guard, for about two hours. Then the Mandarin Chief of Police came back and got ready to interrogate us.

"He took possession of a small office and called us in one after another: first of all the Mandarin Attorney General, and then the Mandarin President of the tribunal. Since neither of them reappeared, I concluded they had had no difficulty in exculpating themselves. I had no doubt that I should do likewise and I fortified my conscience with the evidence of the facts. The three ministers were ushered in, and after them the solicitor and the director of the prison. I was left alone with the executioner and his assistants, the latter quite calm and unruffled, the former immersed in a grim silence."

FIVE

"In my turn I entered the office and confronted the high mandarin. He expressed deep regret at being obliged to have me searched by two of his men. I complied with this formality with a good grace, so impatient was I to get the tedious business over as quickly as possible. The deep pockets of my outer cloak were turned inside out, its thick lining prodded. The sleeves were subjected to a careful scrutiny. Needless to say, the policemen found nothing of an incriminating nature. I breathed more freely. The mandarin looked disappointed. He dismissed his subalterns, made me sit down opposite him, and, after the preliminary remarks dictated by politeness, delivered himself as follows:

" 'Doctor, I'm going to speak to you quite frankly. A murder was committed this morning in the prison of Yi-Ping and the victim is none other than the man who was condemned to death. According to my information, this is not the first but the latest of a long series of attempts on human life, spread out over several months, perhaps several years. I confess, Doctor, that my suspicions first centered on you, given the nature of the weapon employed. So I must ask you a direct question. Was it you who administered the poison?'

"As you may well imagine, sir, these words, although adding to my perplexity, served to dispel my apprehension. I was clearly the object of a definite suspicion and I should be able to exculpate myself with ease. I replied with righteous indignation that I had never administered any poison and had no idea what this was all about. The chief of police thought this over, made a note of my reply, and decided to enlighten me further.

" 'The denunciation sent to the governor,' he explained, 'maintains that capital executions are not being carried out in the proper manner in the city of Yi-Ping, and haven't been for some time. The condemned men are already dead, do you hear? —dead and not just unconscious, at the moment the executioner fulfills his function. The source of this information claims that they are poisoned some time between reveille and the execution. That could only

40

be by the hand of one of the officials. This morning, without your knowing it, I was watching you all closely. I could not detect a single guilty gesture, but I now know that the information is true. The condemned man succumbed to poison and not to the sword. This is against the rules of every civilized country and in particular those of the province of Li-Kang. I have scientific proof of the crime. The condemned man's body has been examined by a medical authority, and the expert is in no two minds about it: death by poisoning. . . . No doubt his was a rather more thorough examination than yours, Doctor,' he added, giving me a nasty look.

"This remark filled me with confusion—I, whose professional honor was untarnished. I had to admit I had been guilty of negligence. My examination of the body had been extremely superficial. I was in a hurry to get it over and done with, and how could I have entertained the slightest doubt as to the cause of death? He that is without sin among us, sir, let him cast the first stone at me!"

"I would not be the one to cast it, venerable sir. Your haste is entirely excusable. Your oversight does not shock me. The question that defeats me is, which of those Chinese officials, which of those mandarins could ever have thought of taking such a step? And by what means?"

"By what means? The details are ghastly. I shudder at the very idea of them, but, while deploring the inevitable shock to a man of your sensibility, I can't conceal them from you.

41

"The poison, so I was informed by the Mandarin Chief of Police, a poison almost unknown in the province of Li-Kang, an extremely violent poison that annihilates its victim a few seconds after its absorption, had been mixed with the drink offered to the condemned man. . . . I'm surprised, sir, not to hear you voice your astonishment at this."

The Chinese doctor uttered these words in a somewhat declamatory tone, and looked at me with an expectant, slightly disappointed expression, like an orator annoyed at having failed to produce the effect he has anticipated.

"The drink?" I said dryly. "I thought as much."

"Sir, I was beginning to envisage that hypothesis myself, for the condemned man had not absorbed any other substance. What surprises me, though, is not that you managed to arrive at the truth entirely through your own resources, but to see you remain so composed and not even shudder with horror, as I did, when I heard the high mandarin methodically explain how some treacherous hand had made a lethal brew of the whiskey, that final favor granted by the humanity of our laws to the wretch who is about to die.

"I see you did not shudder at all. I wonder if your delicate feelings are not assumed and, considering all the fuss you made at first, I'm inclined to charge you with hypocrisy."

His gaze was fraught with protest. I felt I had to justify myself.

"Forgive me, venerable sir, but your story really

42

is very strange; you said so yourself. I find it so disturbing that I can scarcely tell when I ought to feel emotion. This isn't the first time I have gone astray in the process of reasoning, and confused logic with absurdity. You've succeeded in distorting my reactions in matters of sensibility. You see me completely at sea. I shall do my best not to commit a further blunder and to model my feelings on yours. But I wonder into what depths you're leading me."

"Sir, I don't quite understand what you mean. Never mind. From now on I shall stick to the facts."

"That's it, the facts," I earnestly agreed. "No one can be deceived by the facts. There must be some area of agreement between us, centered on the facts."

The old Chinese shrugged his shoulders and went on:

"An analysis of the few drops remaining at the bottom of the cup had confirmed the method used. The high mandarin had then suspected the director of the prison. The whiskey came from his cellar, and he was the one who had handed the cup to the condemned man. But, on being questioned, he had defended himself with such indignation that the police chief was prevailed upon to believe him. Besides, the flagon, still on the table, contained no trace of poison. The poison might have been introduced into the cup by any other hand, but not his. Furthermore, it was impossible to conceive of any motive that might have induced him to take such a step."

"A motive?" I broke in, raising my eyes.

"Yes, sir. The motive. Why do you look at me like that? Surely you know that motive is a fundamental question in all criminal proceedings. In this case there appeared to be none.

"Nor could the chief of police think of any motive for the three ministers. On the contrary, the condemned man had declined their services, and their evident concern was to prolong his life as long as possible in the hope that the approach of his last minute on earth would bring him back to a sense of religion."

"I now admire your logic, venerable sir," I said.

"As for the two mandarin magistrates, he had only questioned them as a formality. It was obvious that neither of them could have the slightest reason to do away with a man condemned to death."

"What amazes me is how that high mandarin could ever have suspected you. I think I'm beginning to get a glimpse of your character, and I don't consider you capable of such a misdemeanor."

"I am grateful, sir, for your opinion. The same thought occurred to me and I respectfully pointed out to the police chief that I, too, had not the slightest motive of hostility against such defenseless wretches. To this he replied that men of science are always ready to try out a new experiment, out of love for their profession, and that just because this poison was so little known I might have thought of using it, as a dangerous test, on a man condemned to death. He went on:

" 'In any case, Doctor, there's at least one charge against you in this affair. As a medical man, you have failed on two counts. You did not state that the condemned man was dead a quarter of an hour before the execution, which is contrary to the ritual. Secondly, you signed a certificate of death by decapitation, which is false. If you did not actually administer or even provide the poison, you are guilty of negligence, and it is in your own interests that I ask you to assist me in discovering the real culprit.'

"We Chinese are extremely punctilious in matters of ritual. A mere accusation of complicity could have got me into serious trouble. I was therefore prepared to do all I could to satisfy him. I carried my thoughts back to my arrival in the dark at the prison. First of all, the officials had assembled in the registry. I had vaguely noticed the flagon of liquor and the cup on the table. Someone had obviously introduced the poison in our absence—someone who had stayed behind in the room during the reveille ceremony. Then, taking into consideration the extraordinary behavior. . . ."

"The executioner!" I exclaimed.

"It stands out a mile. Yes, the executioner, or, at a pinch, one of his assistants. And when I recalled his attitude in the reception room, there was no longer a doubt in my mind. In fact, he had admitted it in so many words. A curious coincidence—the misapprehension that must be attributed to our incomprehensible emotion—had led us to misinterpret the significance of his behavior.

45

"I was blinded by this revelation. 'The executioner!' I exclaimed triumphantly, just as you did a moment ago. Needless to say, the Mandarin Police Chief with his professional lucidity had already come to this conclusion. He was merely trying to study my reactions, for he had not yet discarded the possibility of my complicity. My spontaneity seemed to satisfy him. All the other witnesses must have reacted in the same way. He asked me a few more questions, then dismissed me and called in the principal suspect."

"Our deductions were correct, sir. It was the executioner, all right. His assistants were innocent. Having suspected the crime for some time, they in fact were the authors of the letter of denunciation.

"He repeated his confession. This left no room for ambiguity. He declared that he had always followed this procedure during the three years he had occupied his post. He had thus poisoned seven men who had been condemned to death. Seven murders, sir—a ghastly scandal! This had taken place right in front of my eyes, and I had never noticed a thing. I was therefore equally incriminated at the outset."

"You were equally incriminated?"

"Yes, sir. The executioner himself being unable to explain the motive which had prompted him to commit these acts, and even though he stated that he had acted entirely on his own, there was still some doubt about him in the mind of the high mandarin."

"The motive, I suppose?" I said, looking at him again in perplexity.

"Yes, sir, the motive. The executioner appeared to have no more motive than we did. I warned you, this is a strange story."

S I X

The old Chinese paused for a moment. I kept silent
as I pondered on his story. Eventually he spoke
again, looking at me closely.

"What do you think of my tale, sir? I see you are
lost in thought."

"A number of points bother me," I said. "You
start off with the description of a macabre scene.
You drag me into an obscure misapprehension of
dubious morality. Then your story begins to sound
like a detective novel. You dish up a murder and a
murderer just when they are least expected. To

crown it all, I notice you're not above indulging in dramatics."

"I was sure my story would fascinate you, sir."

"Not at all. You're quite mistaken. I'm criticizing it severely. I enjoy whatever is strange, but all this is gratuitously absurd in the extreme. You promised me simplicity!"

"And I maintain that I've kept my word," the doctor protested in an injured tone. "I maintain that my story is perfectly simple schematically. If you find it absurd, it's merely because you, sir, have lost your common sense. An unexpected murder and murderer, did you say? You haven't even noticed that the victim was determined, marked down as though with a branding iron, from the very start. There's no deception. The victim really is *the victim;* do I make myself clear? And his executioner, you must admit, is none other than *the executioner.* There isn't any *basic* ambiguity anywhere. My story is a crystallization of good sense and straightforwardness."

"Traitor!" I muttered. "Enticer! O you devil, I recognize your insidious, bewitching logic-chopping only too clearly. Yet I had sworn never to be caught up in your snares again. Yes, I admit, I am forced to admit, that the substance of the story is simple. But I should like it to be clearer still, if you see what I mean. I should like its clarity to be evident to the least sophisticated mind, without its necessitating any intellectual effort. I live in a world that doesn't appreciate *chinoiseries.*"

49

"*Chinoiseries,* sir?" said the old Chinese, knitting his brows.

"What I mean is, subtleties. Tell me quite frankly: Is the rest of it sufficiently ordinary, sufficiently commonplace and conventional, for a child of twelve to to able to appreciate its spice at a single reading? If not, it would be better to stop here and now. I promised my guardian angel not to welcome any further suggestions for literary purposes."

"I can assure you on that point. There is no spice in the rest of the story."

"So much the better, venerable sir," I exclaimed, delighted. "Yes, but unfortunately that's still not enough. Unspiciness is necessary, but not sufficient. While listening to you, I've too often had the sensation of sinking into quicksand. Have you finished with these sinister ceremonies, these traps, these cases of *flagrante delicto,* and all this villainous police atmosphere?"

"You can set your mind at rest. From now on the Mandarin Chief of Police is going to vanish from the scene and be succeeded by the mandarin magistrates."

"That doesn't reassure me in the least, venerable sir!" I cried out in dismay. "Mandarins of any sort cannot possibly figure in my stories. Their feelings are always too lofty to make good reading. I should like to follow you, I'm most eager to follow you, but you'll have to cast aside all the characters who represent authority in any way."

"That's asking a great deal, sir."

50

"I'm not the one who's asking it, venerable sir. If it were only myself I had to listen to!"

"I can't cast aside all the mandarins," the old Chinese firmly replied. "In the province of Li-Kang a court of assizes is inconceivable without magistrates."

"A court of assizes? What court of assizes?"

"Isn't that what you call the tribunals that try your criminals? Have I been so boring and unintelligible that you've already forgotten the executioner? His trial constitutes the whole framework of my story. But you are unnecessarily concerned about the mandarin magistrates. They have only a secondary role to play. They are merely there as the representatives of Justice."

"I see. All the same, venerable sir, my head is spinning, and even your promises send a shudder down my spine. You see me on the horns of a painful dilemma."

"Sir," said the old Chinese, "will you kindly stop behaving like a child. Who's in charge here? Your role is to listen in silence—and say thank you afterward. But since that's the way it is, I shan't say another word. My story ends here and now."

"Here and now!"

"The executioner stated he had acted on his own, without an accomplice. In the end they believed him, and I was charged only with negligence and sentenced to pay a small fine. That's all."

"What do you mean, that's all. Why, you promised—!"

"That's all, sir," he repeated stubbornly. "I was only charged with negligence—"

"But I don't care a rap about your sentence!" I exclaimed. "The executioner—what happened to the executioner? Can't you see he's the only one I'm interested in? Don't you realize that maniac is the saving grace of your story, just as other madmen occasionally redeem the sins of the world? You told me he acted without any motive. You gave me to understand that he was tried as a criminal. And you mean to end your story there?"

"The trial was a great sensation, sir, and I could describe it to you in detail, for I was so fascinated by it that I noted it all down. But these *chinoiseries,* to use your own phrase, are unworthy of you. I'm very sorry. The executioner was an extremely peculiar character, quite out of the common run. His career affords some really extraordinary touches, all fresh in my mind and calculated to entrance the amateur of the bizarre whom I mistakenly thought I had found in you. Let's say no more about it."

"You devil! Stop playing with me like a cat with a mouse. I must, I simply must know what happened to that executioner. I must hear the whole story."

Our relationship became somewhat strained. I cursed him up and down. I threatened him. But I soon saw I had nothing to gain by this outburst. In fact, I am certain he was delighted to witness such a display of Western temper. I forced myself to be patient. I humbly apologized. I groveled at his feet and begged him to go on with the story of the executioner. In the end he relented slightly.

"I will certainly go on with the story, since you appear so eager to hear it, but I lay down two conditions."

"I accept them without knowing what they are, venerable sir. Please go on. As for my guardian angel, to hell with him!"

"You seem to be in a more sensible frame of mind at last. These are my conditions. First, since these facts were disclosed by the executioner himself in the course of his trial, I must drag you into those proceedings and, of course, introduce the mandarin magistrates who administered justice to the satisfaction of all concerned."

"It's sheer blackmail, but I said I'd accept it all. You've got the better of me. Drag me into anything you like, even into hell. But go on with your story."

"Secondly, since I suspect you of hyprocrisy and I don't wish to be accused of inflicting a scandalous subject on you by trickery—do you think I am so keen to tell you this story? We shall now take leave of each other. Think the matter over and weigh up your scruples for eight days. I shall be here at the same time next week and bring my notes with me. Remember. In eight days' time."

I cursed my guardian angel, my doubts, and my uncertainties, but I could not press the point. An old Chinese is a difficult muse. This one was a particularly tough nut to crack and required the full deployment of my perfidy. I changed tactics and started discussing commonplaces. He softened, and we left each other on apparently friendly terms, although he did not utter another word of his story. He would rather have been chopped into bits, like the food we had been eating, than make the slightest allusion to it again that evening.

I went off with rage in my heart, feigning indifference.

And as I was leaving the magical city of Yin-Yang in the dark, I came across my guardian angel waiting for me in the moonlight, sitting on a stone and preening the long feathers of his white wings to allay his impatience and curb his anxiety.

He had not dared to venture into the accursed town but, since nothing could be concealed from him, he knew all about my conversation with the old Chinese. He vented his indignation in reproaches, somewhat mitigated by his tone of paternal authority.

"You wished me in hell, you cursed me," he said tearfully. "That I can forgive on account of your extreme youth. But here you are once again on the verge of committing a serious sin. Take heed of my warning, if not out of love for me, then at least out of respect for Literature, over which we stand guard —we, the angels, whom you had promised henceforth to serve faithfully, and to whom the maunderings of that old Chinese with the Mephistophelean countenance are an outrage.

54

"I am prepared, charitably, to turn a blind eye on this latest prank of yours on condition that it does not occur again and that it leaves no written traces. Don't go to the meeting you arranged. Forget that impossible Chinese. One more escapade like this, and you're lost. *Abyssus abyssum invocat.* I have trusted you up to now in spite of your whims, but another lapse will oblige me to abandon you on your downward path and even to rend you asunder."

"Listen," I implored him, "have pity on me. My mind is in a whirl. I feel torn between you and my old Chinese."

"An executioner murdering a condemned man! Can you imagine it? In the first place, it's utterly improbable. I've never read that anywhere before. Secondly, it's irrational, since there's no motive behind it. Finally, even that yellow devil himself was cynical enough to warn you that the man in question was a rather unusual character!

"You must do as I say. I've told you a hundred times before: don't try to distinguish yourself from others—others greater than you have exhausted themselves at that sterile game. Abandon all pretense at research. You're at the age when a writer must guard himself carefully against those unwholesome impulses and concentrate all his energies on attaining the admirable perfection of normal qualities. The true artist can be recognized by his severity, by which I mean the patient genius he deploys to tame the demon of novelty in him and limit the originality of his work to the imperceptible vibrations which, on my charts, record the harmonious progress of the good old state of things."

There was so much benevolence concealed behind these stern words that I could not prevent myself from bursting into tears.

"I shan't do it again!" I cried. "I shall punish that Chinese for his impertinence. I'll leave him to his rattles, his firecrackers, and his chopsticks. I swear I shan't go to that meeting."

My guardian angel's face beamed. He, too, shed tears of joy and gave me absolution. Purified and with a light heart, I returned with him to the world of moderation.

For a whole week, actually, I applied myself to fortifying my mind in its good intentions. For a whole week, yes, I followed my guardian angel's advice to the letter and punctiliously read a number of works he had recommended, feverishly trying to find in them some orthodox characters. For a whole week—I swear—I restricted myself to the company of dull, harmless people, and rushed off at full speed whenever I spied a countenance that differed in the slightest way from that of an average person.

2

SEVEN

And eight days later, almost dying of boredom, I
returned to the magical city of Yin-Yang. I found
myself in the restaurant at the time the Chinese doctor had ordained. What am I saying? My mind was
tortured with remorse, but I was there well ahead of
time!

He, however, turned up at his leisure. He was
carrying a brown leather brief case, which he put
down on the table. He displayed no surprise or satisfaction at seeing me. He greeted me in the Chinese
fashion. I rose to my feet and returned his greeting
automatically.

We were now sitting opposite each other, dipping

our chopsticks into the outlandish food I had ordered on his advice. After the lengthy preliminary small talk prescribed by convention, he told me he had assembled several documents dealing with the executioner's trial. He would be pleased to translate them for me since, apparently, I had decided to hear the rest of the story.

This last remark and the somewhat exaggeratedly courteous tone he had used, even for a Chinese, awakened my sense of dignity.

"Just a moment, venerable sir," I said. "Today it's my turn to lay down certain conditions."

For it would be wrong to take me for a weakling with no determination, ready to surrender without a struggle to all the influences of the present occasion. I had come back to Yin-Yang, I admit, but I had taken precautions. If I had abandoned many of my original objections, if I had ventured rather far along the path of renunciation, there was one point at least at which I would go no farther; beyond this point all the Chinese in the world would not be able to force me.

"I've given proof of my good faith, venerable sir. I have yielded to the fantasy of your reminiscences, but you must make some concession in return. I'll be absolutely firm on this point. If you wish me to listen to your story—and in spite of what you said, I can see that you are just as eager to tell it as I am to listen to it—promise me that it does not offend morality."

"Sir," said the old Chinese, "what do you mean by that?"

I gave the matter considerable thought before replying.

"What I mean is this: Promise me that it is not one of those infernal intrigues wherein Good is indistinguishable from Evil."

"I promise," the old man said.

"Give me your promise as a Chinese gentleman that at no time do the wicked appear to be good or caressed by an insidious ray of light that endows them with a scandalous halo; that the good never behave in a manner to turn one's stomach by arousing a disgust for virtue."

"That's a reasonable request. I give you my word as a Chinese gentleman, sir."

"As in real life—I mean, our sort of life?"

"As in your sort of real life."

"I must go one step further. Will you swear that in your story there's a substantial barrier between vice and virtue?"

"I swear there is."

"As solid, as impenetrable and insurmountable a barrier as in the reality of our world?"

"Just as insurmountable, sir."

"Even that is not enough. You would still be capable of finding a loophole. I'm going to restrict the circle of your obligations with such a brilliant stroke that you won't have the slightest excuse for overstepping it. Swear again, swear by your ancestors, swear that, as in the real world—as in the real world in which I myself am living, do you hear?

61

—it is the wicked on whom the hand of Justice will fall, and not on the good."

"That goes without saying, sir. I swear by my ancestors."

"One last oath, and I'm yours body and soul. Before all the gods in China, swear yet again that farce will not be interwoven with drama, that the grotesque and the tragic will retain their own respective characters and will have no more in common with each other than Good with Evil."

"Sir, I swear it."

"You really mean it—you're not setting a trap? Exactly as in human relations?"

"As in human relations. Is that all?"

"That's all," I said, heaving a sigh of relief. "I can now listen to you with a clear conscience."

"The executioner's trial, sir, began about three months after the scene I've already described, and lasted several days. Let me first give you an idea of the setting.

"By some chance, about which there was nothing peculiar—it was rather an inevitable concatenation of circumstances—the officials playing the leading parts were the very ones who had assembled three months earlier in the prison of Yi-Ping to attend the execution. The Mandarin President of the tribunal occupied the central seat, surrounded by several assistants. The Mandarin Attorney General was seated in the chair reserved for him. The executioner's advocate was also the same as before. As for me, to-gether with the other witnesses of lesser importance, I sat in front of the spectators, just behind the bench of the notables who made up the jury. Our regular presence there was not indispensable, but we had been invited out of politeness.

"We all wore the national costume. That of the officials was in keeping with their dignity. The Mandarin President's robe was richly embroidered and adorned with several bands of rare furs. That of the Mandarin Attorney General, which was bright red, was adorned in the same way, and from the front presented a large escutcheon of a dragon woven in gold and silver. These two dignitaries were likewise laden with necklaces and medals that weighed down their limbs and lent their gestures a ponderous majesty.

"Each of the mandarins was thus attired according to his importance. Each wore a skullcap pierced with a red, blue, or white pin to indicate his rank. Each wore a false beard and false pigtail of a length proportionate to his age. The Chinese have long ago done away with these accessories in everyday life, but they preserve them as symbols of wisdom and vestiges from ancient times. They bring them out on the occasion of a ceremony as important as a Court of Justice. Certain nations of the Western world do likewise, I believe. Each mandarin also wore brightly colored make-up on his face.

"In the semicircle formed by the tribunal, the

notables, and the distinguished guests, only one man, sir, stood out like a sore thumb in this colorful gathering. He was distinguished only by the simplicity of his attire. He was dressed in the coarse drugget suit that the ritual requires. There was no bright paint on his face. Only his forehead had been smeared with white, the color of mourning. It was the accused—the executioner. His name was Chong."

"What did he look like?" I asked.

"To begin with, he looked rather scared. I shall talk about him at greater length later on.

"The courtroom was richly decorated. But I believe you people attach less importance than we do to these artistic effects. I must tell you, though, that the walls were hung with heavy tapestries depicting gigantic dragons. The spaces between were filled with long banners inscribed with black characters— maxims of our greatest sages, carefully chosen to suit the occasion.

"One of these, for instance, stretching from the ceiling to the floor, proclaimed: 'It is an abominable crime to disturb the established order.' Another one read: 'Thou shalt not kill,' and yet another: 'Whosoever takes another man's life is as cruel as the tiger of the forests, and a thousand times more contemptible, for the tiger does not know what he is doing.'

"Now, this is the general procedure with us in this sort of case. The hearing is public. The crowd usually arrives well ahead of time and settles down on the floor opposite the semicircle. Then the accused, his advocate, the distinguished guests, the notables, and, last of all, the Tribunal, take their places. This entry of mandarins is spectacular. A signal is given on the drums and trumpets. The crowd falls silent. Everyone stands up and remains bowed, hands against breast. The accused prostrates himself.

"Then the mandarin magistrates appear in all their pomp, one after another, with arms folded and head lowered in a gesture of meditation. They move slowly and in step. They come to a halt behind the chairs reserved for them. They stand motionless for a moment, turn to the right, then to the left, and ceremoniously greet one another. After that they nod toward the notables, who bow before them. Finally they take their seats and the crowd settles down on the floor again.

"The Mandarin President declares the session open. He is the first to speak. He puts his case succinctly and draws attention to the antecedents of the accused. In China, sir, the magistrates do not simply judge a man by his reprehensible act; they also try to shed some light on his entire life, going as far back as possible into his past, interrogating the members of his family, his friends, and his enemies so as to reconstitute his whole personality.

"This was what was done in the case of the executioner. The Mandarin President devoted the whole of the first part of the morning to an account of Chong's childhood and youth and to filling in the

65

gaps in the original inquiry with various statements of evidence. You will thus have the accused's character sketched out in broad outline for you, just as it was sketched out for us at the beginning of the session."

EIGHT

"This executioner, sir, this fellow Chong, was, as I said before, an extremely odd character, and some of his whims could well lend weight to the argument put forward by his advocate, namely, that he was not fully responsible for his actions.

"Chong was born in Yi-Ping and belonged to an honorable and respected family: a family of executioners. His father, who had died three years before, was an executioner, as his grandfather had been. In China the posts of all mandarins, even the smallest, are hereditary. At this point, I remember, the president made a short digression to evoke his ancestors, render homage to their unblemished name, remind him of the examples he had had before his eyes, and lament at seeing one of their descendants on the bench of infamy.

"He had had a happy childhood, like most little Chinese boys. The statements of evidence covering this period of his life brought nothing remarkable to light, and nothing definite that could be held against him. At most it appeared that he had evinced a certain shyness or oversensitivity that drove him to shun the games of his companions and resort to the society of weaker creatures: women, girls, and even, on occasion, domestic animals, for whom he showed an unusual affection. Though this trait in itself gave no cause for anxiety in such a small child, it should nevertheless be noted that instead of disappearing it became all the more pronounced as Chong grew older. No doubt it was deeply embedded in his nature.

"One of his former companions mentioned an incident illustrating the development of this bent rather well and that the notables, with good reason, considered extremely significant.

"Here is the statement of evidence of this witness:

" 'One day, Mandarin President, I had gone out into the country with a group of friends. Chong joined us, which was unusual, since he scorned our amusements.

" 'During the morning we set some traps of silk

netting and, when I came back to lift mine after lunch, I was lucky enough to find in it, alive, a magnificent one-year-old pheasant. I was extremely proud, naturally, and all the others envied my dexterity. Before taking it out of the netting, I pulled a long needle out of my pocket and prepared to sew up the pheasant's eyelids, the usual method of keeping a captive bird and taming it easily. All my friends shrieked with delight and crowded around me to assist in this operation, eager to watch and admire the feverish palpitations of the golden-plumed bird.

" 'All of a sudden Chong, who had stood apart in silence, broke into the circle. He, usually so calm and placid, flung himself at me, Mandarin President, without my having done anything to provoke him, at the very moment that I was taking careful aim to insert the needle. Such was the violence of his onslaught that I let go of the bird. He snatched it up and with nervous gestures began freeing it from the net. For a moment or two I was too surprised to move, for there was a strange gleam in his eye and he appeared to be in the throes of a violent emotion. Eventually I told him the bird did not belong to him and went up to recover my booty.

" 'Then, realizing he would get the worst of it, for my comrades in their indignation were ready to support me, he took a few steps back, released the bird completely, and flung it high into the air. With anger blazing in his eyes he told us that it did not belong to anyone since he could not keep it for himself. In our righteous fury we gave him a good beating with a stick. But that did not get me back my golden pheasant, and I was deeply grieved.

" 'That is all I have to say, Mandarin President. That act revolted my adolescent heart. Even today I can only ascribe it to sheer spite and jealousy.' "

"So much for this particular witness. Several others made similar statements. But, after all, sir, one knows what these youthful outbursts of temper are like. They were acts of no particular import, which could be blamed on a spoiled childhood. Chong's mother had a weakness for her son and allowed him too many of his whims."

"I understand; the tribunal did not hold it against him?"

"Of course not, sir. What an idea! It was not to torment him that they were delving like this into his past. It was, as I explained, to get as complete a picture as possible of his mentality and to discover all the elements that might have influenced the evolution of his character."

"Your protest reassures me, venerable sir. Please go on. I am impatient to get a clearer picture of his character."

"Chong, sir, never gave any real cause for alarm, and his family began to get anxious only shortly after he came of age, when his father applied for and obtained for him a position as an assistant executioner. This father naturally wanted his son to succeed him. He wanted him to embark on his apprenticeship under his guidance, which is the rule with all artisan families. . . . Have you any children, sir? I mean, have you a son?"

"No children, venerable sir. I take a fairly optimistic view of the fate of humanity, but not to the point of siring a family. No son."

The Chinese doctor thought this over for some time, then gave a sigh and went on in a sententious tone:

"Nor have I, sir, but I think we are both deprived of one of the greatest joys in this world: the joy of seeing another self grow up who will prolong our own existence; the joy of directing his education, of transmitting our knowledge to him, of sparing him the errors into which we fell; the joy of reliving with him our first faltering footsteps, of seeing him hesitate at first, then master himself; the joy of teaching him in a few years what we took half a lifetime to acquire; the joy of seeing him gradually rise to our own level and—this must be profoundly moving—of perceiving that he has equaled us, and of sensing his vaguely trying to surpass our ability in the matters taught him; and the final joy of knowing that our task is accomplished and of becoming the mute and anguished witness of a perfection that disconcerts us."

"You amaze me, venerable sir," I said. "I'm sometimes tempted to believe you have a soul."

"Yes, sir, I've always regretted not having a son. Thus, despite my lack of personal experience, I can imagine as clearly as anyone what the father's despair must have been when he saw that Chong not only

71

showed no inclination for the profession of his ancestors but actually performed his new functions as
though they were an ordeal, appearing to be almost
ashamed of them—rather like those sons of rich mer-
chants who are embarrassed to serve or even be seen
in their parents' shop, forgetting that it is the source
of their fortune and respectability.

"To begin with, of course, he did not dare openly
oppose his father's wishes, but he applied himself to
his task with every sign of ill will. The Mandarin
President quoted actual details, which left no room
for doubt as to his clumsiness, not to say his systematic negligence. After his father reproached him for
his behavior, he so far forgot himself as to reply—
respectfully, it's true—that he did not feel it was a
suitable job for him.

" 'As a matter of fact,' the president here observed,
'it is only too clear that at this period Chong regarded
himself as a creature of superior substance and had
already been tempted by the evil genius of personal
initiative.'

"These initial remarks inevitably shed an unfavorable light on the accused. In China, as you know,
respect for tradition, for what is old and has survived
the test of time, is the basis of all virtue. On points
of detail, certainly, we allow Western practices, especially when we derive an immediate benefit from
them; but our spiritual heritage must remain intact.
In spite of the barbarous doctrines that have inun-
dated us in the course of the centuries, we scarcely
know any other religion than that of 'conservation,'

any other paradise than the citadel of the past. Despite all our dragons and countless jinns, there is only one devil we really dread: the demon of change and novelty."

"That's not possible, venerable sir!" I exclaimed. "I'm absolutely hypnotized. I would never have thought that such a frame of mind could still exist in this world. I can hardly imagine it."

"It does, though, sir. . . . Even as a young man, Chong already appeared to be subject to dangerous impulses, and it was not long before there was no more doubt on that score.

"One day, while dealing with a condemned man who struggled and put up a fierce defense, he gave such a feeble, clumsy, pitiful performance that his father, out of shame for him, had to intervene personally in certain details of the execution that are specifically the assistants' responsibility, thereby losing a certain amount of dignity. The day after this exhibition Chong declared outright that he would not, could not, go on with this sort of job.

"He persisted in this decision with surprising determination, considering his usual lack of resolution, and in spite of the remonstrances, threats, and entreaties of his father who was sick with anguish at the thought of losing face irremediably as a result of this abdication. Nothing would make the son change his mind. The unhappy father therefore cursed his son and turned him out of the house. Then he locked himself up in his room to brood on his grief and humiliation. The wretched man's lot had a profound effect on the tribunal. They rendered homage to his memory."

"I am also deeply moved, venerable sir. But what about Chong? What happened to him?"

"He fled in shame. He was forced to leave Yi-Ping, and even the province of Li-Kang, where he had no friends and where he could find no means of livelihood, his conduct having been severely censured. He disappeared. For the next ten years all trace of him was lost, and the inquiry carried out in the town of Yi-Ping elicited only a few slender clues to this period. All that was known was that he had been in the far south and had had a rather hard time of it. . . ."

"There were several reasons for this, sir," the old Chinese observed, resuming his sententious tone. "He knew no trade that could assure him a reasonable existence in our impoverished provinces. He had been brought up as an executioner, in a family of executioners. One does not with impunity break with traditions, bonds as strong as chains, everything that contributes to the formation of a man's personality. By his own hand he had condemned himself to live as an outcast. And so he languished, without parents, without friends, without means, no doubt in abject poverty, and one day, ten years after his departure, he turned up again in Yi-Ping."

"Just a moment, venerable sir. This executioner interests me even more than you think. I'd like to know what became of him during those years."

"He will tell us himself later on, at the request of the Mandarin President. I'm giving you the facts in

74

the order in which they were presented at the hearing. For the moment it's this president who is speaking, seated in his chair, leaning slightly forward, while a scribe unrolls before him a scroll of paper on which are inscribed the results of the preliminary inquiry.

"Well, Chong came back to his native city. He was in a pitiful condition when he humbly presented himself to his family. His rebellion, sir, had certainly not benefited him. You expressed the wish, in the name of your morality, that the wicked should be punished. No doubt you are feeling a certain amount of satisfaction at this point: he was reduced to skin and bones, in tatters, and covered with sores and dirt. He was dying of hunger.

"He was ready, he said, to submit to his father's wishes and to resume his apprenticeship by his side. He even implored his father to allow him to re-enter the family house—he and his consort together."

NINE

"His consort! Venerable sir, I could hug you for that! God be praised! A woman! Your story, you must admit, was rather lacking in grace and gaiety. At last here's a somewhat less somber touch. You didn't tell me there was a woman in it."

"There is, but don't rejoice too soon. A woman? His wife! At least that is what he called the wretched, degraded creature he had in tow during his long wandering across China. Really, sir, that executioner had a peculiar character and was disturbingly drawn to all that was low. A demon must have possessed him since birth, and it is not surprising he came to a bad end."

"Nevertheless, tell me something about this woman. She interests me despite her abject condition."

"She appeared at the hearing, just for a very short time, because the magistrates deemed it unnecessary to hear such a witness except as a matter of form. But the Mandarin President felt it was worth while, at this point, to give us a rapid picture of her, this description serving to illustrate Chong's abnormal inclinations more emphatically than a lengthy speech. He also made a point of showing how generous, not to say overgenerous, the father had been in allowing him under his roof again together with this unworthy woman.

"You may perhaps know the importance we in China attach to the appearance of our women. A plump woman is an honor for the whole family, whereas a skinny one is regarded as a disgrace to a respectable clan, since she can be got cheaply. Well, Chong's wife, sir, was positively *scraggy* when she turned up in the town of Yi-Ping! Reliable witnesses had described her as a walking skeleton with hardly an ounce of flesh on her bare bones . . . and what flesh, sir!"

"Really, what flesh?"

"We are delicate artists, as you may perhaps have gathered, and all our poets have sung the flesh tints of Chinese women, comparing them to the rosy petals

77

of a flower that a butterfly scarcely dares to brush with its wings. Listen to this:

" 'You are lovelier than an apricot blossom bathed in moonlight; you are all the flowers and all the scents; you are the splendor of the world.' "

"I'm delighted, but not at all surprised, to find you're a poet, venerable sir. But, if I gather correctly, Chong's wife was not at all like a flower."

"Her complexion was leaden, sir. Not the natural white of the hawthorn, but the deathly pallor of a corpse. She, too, was dying of hunger; and besides, she was diseased, diseased in the chest, and her sickly air inspired nothing but revulsion and disgust in anyone who saw her. Furthermore—I've kept the worst to the last—she was blind. *Blind,* do you hear? As you know, we give our women names that extol the sparkle of their eyes, to honor one of their most obvious charms. We christen them 'Moonbeam' or 'Heavenly Star' or 'Sunshine.' Well, the eyes of this woman, sir, were filmed over and emitted not the faintest gleam. They were sightless.

"A diseased, emaciated cripple, and, to crown it all, a stranger—that was the wife he had brought back with him! As to how he had managed, on his long trek all the way from the southern provinces, to drag her, push her, and carry her along, he subsequently gave a brief summary; but that mystery was never solved completely. Anyway, there she was, by his side, like an insulting challenge to the harmony of this world, when he presented himself to his father like a repentant son. . . . And he wouldn't hear of being separated from her. Her admission into the bosom of his family was the condition he made for his own return to the hearth. In spite of his parents' entreaties he categorically refused to renounce her— he claimed to have married her legally—although he had every right to do so, for her disease was obviously incurable. He was barely prevailed upon, subsequently, since it was clear she would never bear him a child, to yield to his father's pleas and take a concubine. Even then it was only with extreme reluctance that he consented to this, and he did not keep her very long. . . . I am not playing any tricks on you, sir. I warned you this was a strange story despite its simplicity—scarcely credible at times, precisely because of the peculiarity of this executioner, this fellow Chong."

"Venerable sir," I said, "I can understand your indignation only too well. I feel just as indignant as you do. I would give anything for this woman to have been attractive. But you have told me enough about her for me to be able to judge her unworthiness. My curiosity is satisfied for the time being. Don't give me any more horrible details about this ill-favored creature."

"You are right. She was an outrage to Nature, and that's enough.

"Well, the father relented and took them both in. One could perhaps construe this open-handed gesture as a sign of weakness. But you must not forget that to him the return of his repentant son was a glorious compensation and to a degree wiped out the stain inflicted on his honor ten years earlier. Chong, moreover, must have been aware of this and was probably practicing a sort of blackmail. The father accepted the humiliation of such a daughter-in-law as a lesser evil. We've no right to stand in judgment upon him.

"He went even further. He saw to it that she was well-treated under his roof. Thanks to his authority, she escaped the practical jokes she would have had to endure in any other family for the handicap of such a vile personal appearance. Neither her mother-in-law nor the other women in the house employed her as a slave. On the contrary, following the orders given by the head of the family, who wanted her at all costs to put on a little flesh, they absolved her of the more arduous household duties and went out of their way to cook enormous meals for her in the hope of ending the perambulating shame of her skeleton-like limbs. All this led to nothing. She remained as skinny as ever and was still skinny at the time of the trial—skinny and, of course, blind."

"Such, sir, more or less, was the opening address of the Mandarin President. He spoke with complete impartiality. He maintained the attitude of objectivity demanded by his office, and confined himself to the facts. These were significant enough in themselves and needed no further comment. The accused's past appeared in a somewhat disturbing light. The Mandarin Attorney General had given several nods of

disapproval. Counsel for the defense looked apprehensive.

"The president asked the accused if he had any
objection to raise on the grounds of inaccuracy, or
any remark to make on what had been said about
him and his wife. Chong could not very well deny
what was known to the whole town, and made a gesture to indicate that he had nothing to say.

"Then, sir, the second stage of the trial began.
Since you have expressed your curiosity about them,
you will now hear Chong himself describe some of his
adventures."

TEN

The old Chinese opened his brief case and took out several scrolls.

"I have here," he said, "a more or less complete summary of the evidence. What prompted me to take these notes was the sensation caused by Chong's initial replies and the amazement at discovering the ingenuous and insane lengths to which that creature went to provide weapons against himself.

"Even today, sir, the reasons for this blindness are by no means clear to me. I know he had sworn to tell the truth—this practice, which you apply to witnesses, is extended by us to the accused—but no magistrate has ever expected a criminal to abide by his oath in such a rigorous manner when the truth is harmful to his cause. It's true that the most hardened criminals are sometimes seized by a sort of madness that impels them to debase themselves, to make themselves out even more infamous than they appear to themselves in the terror and remorse of solitude. The annals of the judiciary cite cases of this madness, but no one had yet seen such a spectacular example of it.

"The defense, of course, could find in this very excess a fairly plausible argument for irresponsibility. . . . Perhaps, after all, the truth is to be found in that direction? Perhaps Chong already felt he was lost and imagined that only the extravagance of his conduct could save him from the sword. Perhaps this insistence on blackening himself was nothing but the supreme cunning of a quick-witted criminal trying to pass himself off as a madman. I'm not quite convinced, all the same, sir, even though I saw and heard him. I don't think he was clever enough to put on such a show. I am rather inclined to think that he was not even aware of the effect produced by his words."

The old Chinese fell silent for a moment, contemplating these visions of the past with an air of perplexity. Then he shook his head and went on:

"I'll leave it to you to judge. Listen to the conversation that took place between him and the Mandarin President after the usual interrogation to establish his identity."

He unrolled one of the scrolls and read to me from his notes, commenting on them as he went:

"The Mandarin President began by asking the question that neeed answering most urgently of all:

" 'Tell us, Chong, why you came back to Yi-Ping. Why, after showing such a spirit of rebellion ten years earlier, did you implore your father to let you resume your functions as an assistant executioner?'

"To this Chong replied:

" 'I wanted to become an executioner myself.'

"This, sir, caused stir and gave rise to a certain amount of doubt as to his frankness, considering his former tendencies. When the Mandarin President expressed his surprise, Chong added:

" 'I wanted to become an executioner in order to perform the task more quickly.'

"At this point his advocate intervened. He could see the danger only too clearly. He hurriedly explained that his client meant to say: 'I wanted to equal, I even had the ambition of surpassing, by dint of application and dexterity, all the previous executioners, my predecessors, my ancestors.'

"But the Mandarin Attorney General in his turn intervened in the debate. He did not believe, he said, that Chong's words could be construed in this manner. He begged the president to make him explain himself more clearly. Chong looked around the courtroom. He listened, without appearing to understand, to the words his advocate whispered in his ear. He pulled himself together and finally declared:

" 'I wanted to put the condemned man to death before the door of the registry was opened.'

"At that moment the drums went into action for the first time since the beginning of the hearing."

"So the brass band was still there?"

"Yes, sir. Drums and bells. The musicians were concealed behind a curtain, waiting to emphasize any sensational piece of evidence. And this particular statement was soul-stirring, I assure you. It was a confession of *premeditation*.

"As soon as the din died down, the president asked:

" 'How could such a scheme have ever entered your head, Chong? How and when?'

"This brought the executioner up short. He pondered on the question for some time and finally began speaking, cudgeling his brains for the right word as though he found it difficult to express himself. His statement was rather muddled and the president had to unravel it more than once. This is what he said:

" 'It happened a year before my return to Yi-Ping, Mandarin President, more than a thousand li from here, down in the south, in a small town in Yunnan. . . . Yes, that's it, that's where the idea occurred to me.

" 'I was in extreme need. My wife and I were dying of hunger.'

"You will note, sir, that he had already saddled himself with that wretched creature. She was not involved in guilt, but it was made clear very shortly

85

that she had been partly responsible for all his acts. . . .

" 'We had already been through a long, extremely long, period of suffering,' he went on. 'We were at the end of our tether, without hope, and in utter destitution. I saw my wife slowly wilting away before my eyes. I could no longer bear the sight. I decided to put her out of her misery, to make her swallow poison and then take some myself.'

" 'What poison?' the Mandarin President inquired, with a slight start.

" 'I had a bottle with a black label. Someone had once given it to me.'

" 'Was it by any chance,' the Mandarin President asked in a rather unsteady voice, 'was it by any chance the same poison you used later on?'

" 'Yes, it was the same, Mandarin President.'

" 'In your own interests, Chong,' said the president, silencing the murmur of the crowd with an imperious gesture, 'you had better tell the whole truth. How did you come to be in possession of this poison?'

" 'That's easy, Mandarin President. I remember quite clearly. I had worked for a time in the country, at a healer's. I was employed as his servant. He was very fond of me. He died during an epidemic that ravaged the southern provinces. Shortly before his death he sent for me, thanked me for having served him so loyally, and presented me with this bottle. He warned me that it contained a deadly poison that he himself had concocted. He added, I remember, that

86

he could not think of a more precious gift to make to a man like me.'

" 'What did he mean by that?' asked the Mandarin President, voicing the general curiosity.

" 'I don't know what he meant, Mandarin President. He had always been a good master, but he liked to tease me now and then, and he used to laugh at me when I brought home injured birds and shared my food with them. He died an hour later. I thought his mind was already wandering when he uttered those words and I paid no attention to them.

" 'But I religiously kept the bottle to remind me of him. I thought of it when I had no more strength to endure my misery a moment longer.'

" 'In the absence of any further evidence the tribunal accepts your explanation as to how the bottle came to be in your possession. Proceed, Chong, and don't omit a single detail. So you wanted to do away with yourself?'

" 'That was my idea, Mandarin President. I had been thinking about it for several weeks. That evening I made the decision, for myself, for my wife, and also for a wretched animal—a sick dog I had picked up the year before, just as its master was about to have it put away. The man had given it to me in exchange for a handful of rice. I had enough to eat at that time; but for the last few weeks we had been living from hand to mouth, and the fate of that wretched animal added to our torment.

" 'I was therefore determined to end it all that evening. I took the bottle out of its hiding place.'

" 'Was this with your wife's consent?'

" 'Yes, Mandarin President. She had resigned herself to dying with me and the dog. We had nothing left in the world, and the landlord was going to turn us out of our hovel next day, to keep his pigs in it.

" 'My idea was to start off with the dog. I didn't quite know the strength of the poison; I wanted to try it out on him. I poured a few drops out at random into a cup. I added a little water and offered the poor beast the mixture. I turned aside. His plaintive look touched my heart. I can't bear the sight of suffering, Mandarin President. He had become extremely weak. He barely had enough strength to lift his head. My wife was in much the same condition.

" 'With an effort he lapped up the drink. A few seconds afterward I heard a short whine. Then silence. I had to summon up all the courage I possessed to look around.

" 'The dog was lying on his side. It had happened very quickly. A moment before, he was whining; now he was dead. He hadn't suffered, I'm sure of that. It was plain to see. A nervous twinge, an internal spasm that had accounted for the whine, just as an exclamation betrays our surprise when we bite into a sour apple; a second's giddiness, and that's all. The eyes had lost the pained expression that had cut me to the heart. The muzzle, now that the jaws were unclenched, no longer gasped from straining for breath. I felt a great relief to see him lying there like that, Mandarin President.' "

* *

The Chinese doctor interrupted his tale to add a few explanatory comments.

"I don't know, sir, whether, despite my efforts, I've succeeded in giving you a faithful description of Chong's attitude and the impression it made on the crowd. He had implicitly admitted his base intention in the most natural tone, as though unaware of the import of his words, himself destroying the only extenuating circumstance that a generous mind could conceivably allow him: enthusiasm for his profession. He was suggesting, on the contrary, that he had chosen this executioner's job simply for the purpose of killing.

"He now described this ghastly scene as though he were reliving it in a dream, without manifesting the slightest repugnance. Whereas we were all deeply affected, not of course by the death of the dog, but because we vaguely discerned, though they were still wrapped in a fog, the seeds of criminal thought peeping through, he on the other hand did not realize how this factor told against him. I scrutinized him closely at that moment. I can still see him now. There he stood, unaware of the horror of his words, motionless, indifferent, detached and uncomprehending, isolated in the midst of a seething, murmuring crowd . . . a really incomprehensible creature, sir."

"Incomprehensible, venerable sir. Don't try, please don't try to understand him. Don't let yourself be sidetracked by the difficulties of interpretation. Go on with your story. What did he say? What did he do?"

"He now seemed to be in a state of hypnosis. His

pupils were distended and his gaze was fixed on a point in the ceiling above the mandarin magistrates, as though contemplating a vision. Nevertheless he answered all further questions.

" 'Are we to understand, Chong, that the death of this animal exercised an influence on the acts for which you are appearing before us today?'

" 'I'm not quite sure . . . I think it may have, Mandarin President, but I must tell you everything in the right order. I was all prepared to kill myself. The terror I felt at the thought vanished at the state of peace suggested by this corpse. It seemed simple and easy. I seized a basin. I half-filled it with hot water—we had not had any tea for a long time. I was going to pour the poison in—twice as much as I had given the dog. We had agreed, my wife and I, to share the deadly brew. I tilted the bottle. . . .

" 'At that moment, Mandarin President, I had a vision: a sort of dream, though I was wide awake. I had covered the dog's body with my old coat, yet I could still see his placid eyes with their sight snuffed out. It was still the same dog, and yet it wasn't. I saw before me . . . it's difficult to explain, Mandarin President. I saw before me a man condemned to death—the last one, the one over whom I had proved so clumsy before my departure from Yi-Ping. I was spellbound by the man's eyes. I felt as though I were being sucked down with a ghastly whirl into the dark abyss of his distended pupils, while my colleagues slit his robe and tied his hands together. Not a single detail of his face escaped me. His complexion was the color of the mists that rise from certain swamps. The door of the registry was thrown open and I could feel every tremor in his body, for it was my arm that supported him on the way to the scaffold. My own heart was pounding in unison with his. I experienced, Mandarin President—I experienced the full horror of that final quarter hour, from the opening of the registry door right up to the end—the final quarter hour, and the one minute's silence.' "

ELEVEN

"While I'm about it, sir," said the old Chinese, "it might be as well if I described in greater detail the ceremonial of this final quarter of an hour."

"Absolutely unnecessary," I said, shaking my head emphatically. "I've got enough imagination to picture it. Don't lose the thread. You're on the right track. Read me the words of that strange executioner."

"He expatiated, with a certain amount of obscurity, on his hallucination—for that's what it was, there was no doubt in our minds about it.

" 'I can't express it clearly, Mandarin President. I was looking into the very soul, the bare soul of the condemned man; and there was also the dog with its eyes at peace and its limbs at rest. There was nothing else, I assure you, nothing else. . . .

" 'And this vision arrested my arm. It crucified me. And all of a sudden I found myself contemplating it with different eyes. For no apparent reason, I felt a shiver up my spine that was no longer the manifestation of my horror . . . I can't explain, Mandarin President. All I know is, this vision put me into another frame of mind and dispelled any intention I had of suicide. I was now sure, yes, I was sure, that life had not come to an end as I had thought a few moments before. I was standing upright, as though supported by some invisible hand, all my muscles flexed by some mysterious power. To live now seemed like a duty, a duty as imperative as veneration of one's ancestors—to live, Mandarin President, to live and return as quickly as possible to Yi-Ping.

" 'I put the bottle down and carefully recorked it.'

"We had all listened to this statement in complete silence, sir, and of course we were prepared for the question that followed:

" 'Was it at that moment that you made up your mind to resume your career as an executioner?'

" 'Yes, Mandarin President. Yes, I think so,' Chong replied.

"Then, sir," the old Chinese went on, running his finger along the cabalistic signs inscribed on his scroll, so as not to miss a single one, "then the Mandarin Attorney General intervened. He rose to his feet and asked the president for permission to put a question to the accused. His request was granted. Chong twisted around slightly to face this new interrogator. The attorney general spoke in a solemn voice.

" 'The accused has told us enough so that we can hazard a guess as to his true intentions. It is now time he expressed himself without ambiguity. I ask him to describe what idea he had in mind when he recorked that bottle—carefully, as he informed us. Had he already determined his future line of action? Had he made up his mind to murder those condemned to death by giving them poison, as we are entitled to assume? Did he return to his home and resume his duties solely with that aim in view, as his successive statements suggest?'

" 'Objection!' his advocate exclaimed. 'I object formally—'

" 'But why?' Chong put in, with greater alacrity than one would have suspected from him. 'I can answer perfectly well. On the contrary, I thank the Mandarin Attorney General for having enlightened me by asking me this question. I don't think I had ever thought about it seriously. Without assistance I am incapable of solving the simplest problem. It has suddenly just become clear as daylight. I can see it now: the whole plan had naturally taken shape in my head at that very moment—the whole plan, except for a few details, which I worked out on my return journey. It was this plan that had taken the place of the dead dog and the condemned man with the glazed eyes. It was this idea that upheld me and drove me forward on my homeward path and gave me the strength to overcome all the terrible obstacles I encountered.'

" 'That will be all,' said the Mandarin Attorney General, sitting down again. 'There's a clear-cut answer for you. The court ought to be satisfied.'

"You can imagine how satisfied the court was, sir! I can see it all again as though it was only yesterday. The atmosphere was charged with horror. The revelation of such perversity, the frank admission of such cold-blooded calculation had caused a sensation. Not only was there nothing in Chong's voice that expressed the slightest remorse, but his eyes were gleaming like a fanatic's. This foul scheme, which a morbid hallucination had suggested to his mind, he appeared to regard with pride—as a mystic revelation inspired by heaven to enable him to work out his salvation. Yes, sir. An inveterate sinner, suddenly discovering a line of conduct that would put an end to his successive reincarnations and enable him to melt into the universal spirit, would not have spoken in more ecstatic tones than he did in describing the impulse that had driven him back along the roads of China to go and assassinate poor wretches in prison!

"The whole courtroom was appalled. Some of your compatriots maintain that the Chinese are incapable of emotion. If you had seen us at that moment, sir, you would have realized the folly of such a statement."

"I *can* see you," I exclaimed, "I can see you all absolutely clearly!"

"It's when memories of this sort come back to mind, sir, that I go so far, I admit, as to imbibe a little alcohol."

His emotion was quite genuine. He asked me almost humbly for permission to interrupt his story for a few minutes. I granted him this respite all the more willingly, for his tale was beginning to disturb me too, despite my cast-iron mental constitution.

After mastering his feelings, he continued:

"All the officials, although hardened by their association with the criminal mind, were astounded and scandalized by such cynicism. His advocate, having lost face, had nothing more to say. He hung his head. The president, a very wise, experienced old mandarin, probably for the first time in his life abandoned his judicial composure. He was unable to control himself. He burst out, sir, as though he were one of the parties concerned and not a disinterested arbiter. For a moment even his robes were all awry. Picture him in your mind. An angry flush shows through his make-up and his false pigtail lashes the air from left to right. Listen to his words:

" 'But, after all, Chong, if an evil instinct drove you to murder, why did you have to gratify it on men condemned to death? I accept, I don't excuse, but I can conceive of homicidal mania. I have known creatures who were destined for crime from birth. But if killing was an irresistible urge in you, why in the name of heaven did you not attack the first person you came across? Why, when you already possessed the poison, did you have to embark on that long and arduous journey? Why did you pick on victims already crushed by Destiny? Why this particular choice, which I find even more repellent than the act itself?'

" 'Mandarin President,' Chong's advocate broke in, 'I would like this to be recorded as proof of my client's irresponsibility. He is suffering, it's clear, from a twisted mind, a fixed idea, characteristic of insanity. He is no ordinary murderer. He attacks only a special kind of individual. He has never used his poison on anyone else.'

" 'Perversity is certainly not an indication of insanity,' the attorney general retorted.

" 'Answer the question, Chong,' the Mandarin President persisted. 'We want a complete explanation. Why did you aim *solely* at men condemned to death?'

" 'Why—?' Chong repeated hesitantly, rather baffled by this outburst and trying hard to think. 'Why? That's another question I never asked myself. I'm not very clear in my mind on that point.'

" 'Might it not be, Chong, the extreme facility afforded to an executioner to strike down that sort of victim?' the Mandarin Attorney General suggested.

" 'There's certainly something in what you say,' Chong replied. 'It did, in fact, seem so easy, so natural. I often wondered, I remember, why the thought had never occurred to me before, why no one else had ever had the idea. . . . That's absolutely correct,

97

Mandarin Attorney General. I must thank you for clearing the matter up in my mind,' he went on, as though deeply relieved at having at last solved this problem. 'Just think! The alcoholic drink that is handed to the condemned man to give him courage, and just before the final quarter of an hour, too! A mere gesture was all that was required. It was childishly simple. Yes, that's exactly what tempted me.' "

"At these words, sir, the assembly manifested its disapproval by an angry murmur and even by loud exclamations that drowned the voice of the accused. It was late in the day and everyone's nerves were frayed. The Mandarin President proposed an adjournment. The interrogation had not lasted very long, but the importance of the statements made up for its brevity. The Mandarin Attorney General agreed, but not before pointing out that Chong's cold-blooded reasoning was not by any means indicative of insanity. This was so evident after his reply to the last question that his advocate found nothing to say in his defense.

"The hearing was therefore adjourned for that day. The Mandarin President later confessed that he had needed the whole night to recover his serenity.

"Let us follow the example of that sage, sir, and have a short respite, for I can see you are deeply moved. . . . Perhaps I was wrong to dwell at such length on the infamy of this scoundrel. Like all your compatriots, you will probably now make a sweeping generalization and judge all Chinese by the peculiar mentality of a single individual. Don't do so, I beg you. On the contrary, you ought to regard the general reprobation provoked by his conduct as a striking proof of the instinctive horror that vice inspires in us."

T W E L V E

The maintenance of our cordial relations demanded a few words of encouragement on my part. I said to him:

"Venerable sir, you deserve a vote of thanks, for, contrary to what I feared, you're not trying to portray vice in glowing colors. The indignation inspired in your people by the ignominy of this fellow Chong sets my mind completely at rest as to the Chinese sense of morality. Please go on if you are not too tired."

He appeared flattered and proceeded with his tale without further ado.

"On the following day, sir, as soon as the hearing opened, Chong, at the president's request, went on with his story from where he had stopped.

" 'I put the bottle away, Mandarin President, with fingers that still trembled but with my heart infused with fresh courage. The images up till then had blinded my eyes to the squalor of the hovel. When they were dispelled, I noticed my wife's anxious face turned toward mine and I discerned an unvoiced question in her features. She is blind but she can sense a mood, and mine must have intrigued her. I recovered complete control of myself. I described my vision. It seemed to make a deep impression on her. She agreed with me that I should start off for Yi-Ping as soon as possible and resume my career. . . .'

" 'You revealed your intention to her,' the president interrupted in dismay, 'and she did nothing to restrain you?'

" 'I simply told her my dream, as I told it to the court yesterday, Mandarin President, but even without being told she could feel the impulse that was driving me. The whole plan was agreed upon between us, without her requiring any explanation. On the contrary, she encouraged me in my decision. She, too, appeared to derive fresh strength from it. She got up, came over toward me, and we remained close together for a long time, without speaking, holding hands, weeping, and giving thanks to heaven for having wrought a transformation in our hearts. It was a great joy to feel supported in this way.'

"This declaration caused great astonishment. On

101

further reflection, the consensus of opinion was that Chong, having realized he had made an unfavorable impression on the judges the day before, was now trying to redeem himself by laying part of the responsibility on this cripple. That opinion, I think, was mistaken. He must have been telling the truth. If he himself were capable of acting without external influence, this creature (a mere glance at her was enough) could very well have fallen in with any unnatural suggestion. Perhaps she was the only woman in the whole of China base enough for that. . . . And chance had brought these two creatures together, sir—chance or else an incomprehensible whim of a mysterious fate which Westerners, I believe, do not accept."

"Yes, they do," I said. "Only they lump them all together under the name of Providence."

"Be that as it may, the president cut short any possible sly maneuver on the part of the accused. He told him in no uncertain terms that it was not the court's intention to throw the guilt upon a woman, a woman who was ill and blind. Chong heeded this warning with every appearance of the deepest respect and went on:

" 'Having decided to stay alive, Mandarin President, we first of all had to find a means of doing so. We had nothing in the world but the rags we stood up in and a couple of handfuls of stale rice. We could hardly crawl and we wanted to set out for the north the very next day. We had to have something to eat.

102

We looked around to see what we could find. We ate the dog. . . .'

"What's troubling you now, I wonder?" the old Chinese asked, peering at me from under his eyelids, which were screwed up in astonishment. "Oh, I see. The poisoned meat? They both thought of that, which proves they had recovered full possession of their faculties. They threw away all the animal's guts and roasted the rest of the body for the whole night, hoping that the cooking would render the poison harmless. It was a risk that had to be taken; they had to eat. On that point they won: they suffered no ill effects from it."

"I hadn't even thought about the poison. But to eat that dog!"

"I think your sensitivity on that score is somewhat misplaced. In China, where this story takes place, dog flesh is considered a most acceptable food. Eating a dog entails no sense of shame for us, and Chong could not incur any reproach from his judges for that particular act. So we were extremely surprised to see his eyes overflow with tears as he recalled that memory. He, who until then had been intolerably calm and collected, now seemed to be suffering an untimely pang of remorse. This fellow Chong, sir, was to disconcert us like this right up to the end of his trial, without prejudice to the horror he inspired in us. Not one of his reactions was that of a normal Chinese. Don't think I'm taking pleasure in inventing paradoxes; his attitude really was like this. He muttered a few words about this animal he had picked up, then burst into tears."

"I wouldn't dream of accusing you of gilding the truth, venerable sir. I am with you all the way, and without any reservations. Among all the oddities, which are my daily bread and which, as I can see, abound under the skies of China, you have found the ones most likely to satisfy my needs."

"I'm glad of that, sir, though I don't quite understand your enthusiasm. But we now reach the point where our two pilgrims set out for the province of Li-Kang—on foot, of course, because they had no money. An insane project. Chong described this episode in minute detail, which I shall merely summarize for you:

"Next morning, after eating as much as they could, and taking away the half-charred remains of the dog wrapped up in a rag—their only possessions in this world—this cripple who could hardly stand and he, himself unsteady on his feet, cut two sticks from a hedge and set off along the dreadful roads of Yunnan, making their way toward an inhospitable country covered by lofty mountains. They embarked without a second thought on a journey of more than a thousand li. . . . I almost forgot!—in that old rag which served them as a knapsack, there was also the bottle of poison.

"This bottle, sir—he hadn't forgotten it, you may be sure! When he spoke of it a look of ecstasy came over his face. You would have sworn that for him, for both of them, it was a treasure more precious than gold; that it contained within its depths a miraculous elixir capable of giving sacred significance to the shameful extravagance of their scheme, a philter sufficiently potent to make them forget their past suffering and enable them to triumph over every ordeal to come. They had taken infinite precautions so that it should not get broken and so that not a drop should leak away: childish precautions that in any other circumstance might have provoked a smile. Chong described them to us in solemn detail.

"They had manufactured a tight-fitting cork from a knob of wood with a bit of cloth wound around it. This had not been sufficient to allay their anxiety. They had used the last two wretched handfuls of rice to make a paste. This they smeared around the neck of the bottle so as to make sure it was watertight. Then they—I say 'they,' sir, because she helped him —this monster of a woman was now taking part in his insanity. Make no mistake about it, he was quite honest in describing her eagerness as equal to his own— they had worked part of the night on weaving an armature of split bamboo, like those you sometimes find around precious bottles. And to safeguard this infernal potion still further, they had bundled the whole thing up in the still raw and bleeding skin of the dog: the skin from which they could have made a little money! Thus, to gratify their desire, they used up the sum total of their meager resources. The evil powers that had taken possession of their minds inspired them with diabolical ingenuity.

"I saw you smile just now, when I spoke of an

elixir or philter. Having received a modern education, I understand and share your skepticism. But if the truth be told, every now and then ancient legends cross my mind in spite of myself. I find myself dreaming that the country healer who gave him the present might well have been a sorcerer and that he had added to the liquid a magic distillation as pernicious to the mind as to the body. You would excuse these maunderings if you had heard this fellow Chong accounting to us for his strange behavior with painstaking care and describing, in tones that I cannot hope to reproduce, the throes he suffered at the thought that this bottle might be destroyed.

"In spite of my imperfect description, can't you visualize them all the same, just as I can imagine them myself? Can't you see them embarking on that dreadful journey, of whose perils they are well aware, with their shapeless parcel on their backs, impelled solely, according to Chong's own statement, by the desire to kill?"

"I can see them, venerable sir," I exclaimed fervently. "I can see them both. I would be able to see them even if I were blind, and I would never be able to forget them. I don't need the use of my eyes for that. The forcefulness of your description is like an inward illumination. I can see them, I tell you. Your story is getting better and better."

T H I R T E E N

He acknowledged this homage with a bow and unrolled some more scrolls.

"Chong described his journey in detail, sir, first of
all in reply to the president's questions, then carried
away by his recollection of it. He seemed, in the end,
to derive great relief from getting it off his chest.
This lasted during several sessions, and the tribunal
listened to the whole of his tale with customary pa-
tience and with the zest of interest to which his initial revelations had given birth.

"The journey lasted the best part of a year and
was dreadfully arduous. I'm afraid I would tire you

if I recounted all the catastrophes that occurred. Most of them, in fact, offer very little food for your curiosity. They are adventures that inevitably happen to travelers of that sort, adventures whose essential repercussions on human nature can always be summed up in the same monotonous words: poverty, hunger, thirst, fatigue, and fear."

"Poverty, hunger. . . . Do they all have the same flavor, then?"

"Almost all, sir."

"Venerable sir," I said, "your story has not been very cheerful, and here you are announcing further miseries. Yet I'm weak enough to be interested in these repercussions that you seem to despise, of adventures in human nature: these interferences between chance events and organized consciousness. Aren't there any that are likely to throw your hero's character into sharper relief?"

"Some of these incidents, on the contrary, make him appear even more incredible."

"That's what I meant, venerable sir."

"Let me see now . . . there's one, in particular, that you might like to hear, because there's an element of comedy about it for a change."

"A comic incident, venerable sir? Quick, tell me about it."

"Here it is. It's the story about the brigands who. . . ."

"Venerable sir!"

I had shuddered as I thought I had discerned, in the heavy atmosphere of the restaurant, the rustle of wings whereby my guardian angel announces his presence. I must have been mistaken, for he never ventures into the city of Yin-Yang; but my dormant scruples were roused as a result.

"Venerable sir," I implored, "a story about brigands! And after the detective novel, too! Just as I was beginning to believe you were on the right track! You're going back to the turgid stream of implausible vulgarity. From the standpoint of literature, brigands are impossible."

But the old man asked me, in a rather sharp tone, not to start fussing all over again. Our relations, which had improved considerably, were in danger of becoming strained once more. I did not have enough strength to embark on a fresh quarrel. I took refuge in my cowardice and let myself be carried a little further along the forbidden path. In any case, he had already resumed his story, without paying further attention to me.

"It was a month after their departure, sir, that this incident occurred. You must take my word for it— I'm the first to deplore the fact—but brigands still exist in China, and certain provinces in the south are infested with them, especially the part of Yunnan our two pilgrims had to cross. Our honor and our dignity are not affected by this rabble, for they are not countrymen of ours but belong to a number of barbarian tribes which at one time came down from Tibet. That does not keep them from holding up Chinese travelers just the same.

"Up till then Chong and his consort had been traveling through a fairly fertile and relatively civilized region: the plateau of Yunnan. There are plenty of farmsteads there. In one or another of them they had always been able to find a sheltered corner to spend the night, and even a little food after they had gnawed the last bones of the dog. Although they were unsuited to rural labor and unable to provide anything else in exchange for this skill, they managed here and there to glean a handful of rice or the remains of a meal, enough to keep body and soul together. The Chinese are kind-hearted people, sir.

"Their luck changed when they came to the end of the plateau and reached the mountains that cover northern Yunnan. That's where the kingdom of the brigands starts. The few cultivated fields that are still to be found in the foothills are guarded night and day by the militia. A little farther on it is all forest, intersected only by a few steep paths where travelers never venture except in convoy and with an armed escort. For all these precautions, they are frequently attacked.

"Chong and his consort, however, did not hesitate to set off alone across this wilderness that barred their path. They could not join a convoy. The pace of the mules and foot travelers was far too fast for them. The blind woman stumbled at every step, which is hardly surprising, for these paths, dotted with potholes and rocks, are hard going even for a man in possession of all his physical faculties. Chong was obliged to guide and support her constantly, so that they progressed at the speed of a tortoise. And they had a journey of a thousand li before them!

"So there they were, stumbling up the first slopes. As a matter of fact, the brigands were the least of their worries. This is not hard to understand. The latter do not usually attack wayfarers who are completely destitute.

"Yet they were held up all the same. They thought they had nothing on them to arouse anyone's rapacity, apart from a few meager provisions begged from the farms before leaving the plateau. They were mistaken, sir. There was the bottle! That mysterious bottle, full of a colorless liquid like alcohol and wrapped up with a wealth of precautions which made it look like a precious flagon—the brigands were going to seize it in the hope of a carousal.

"This is where the comic incident I promised you occurs. Chong, who had surrendered all their food supplies without lifting a finger, although those few handfuls of rice and manioc represented several days of continued existence, suddenly snatched up the bottle, leaped away, took up a position with his back against a tree, and defied his assailants. He flatly refused to pay this ransom, saying that he would rather be killed, and his consort with him. (It's a great pity, moreover, that the brigands didn't kill him!) He took a firm grip on his stick, he told us, ready to defend his bottle to the death, and the wretched cripple he called his wife placed herself at his side, imitating the threatening attitude (these are his own words) of her husband. This is how he described it:

" 'We felt endowed with superhuman strength, Mandarin President, and capable of dealing with any foe. We were not in the least afraid. We brandished our sticks in such a fearsome way that the bandits were intimidated and abandoned the notion of robbing us.'

"In such a fearsome way! Can you picture the scene, sir? That band of lawless and godless ruffians, armed to the teeth—can you imagine them being *intimidated* by the grotesque demonstration of those two decrepit creatures reduced to a shadow by their privations? You can't believe it: a mere child would have had them at his mercy. To hear him give this mystifying description, you might have assumed, and with good reason, that the brigands had been disarmed not by their belligerent attitude but by the irresistible laughter that seized them, as it seized the assembly and even the tribunal at the mention of such an outrageous absurdity. . . . Doesn't it make you laugh, sir?"

"Don't bother about me, venerable sir. I'm laughing inwardly. That's a habit of ours in the West."

"It was to this laughter, almost certainly, that they owed their salvation. For, it's a fact, the brigands agreed to leave them their bottle and not molest them any more. Their leader, however, laid down a condition. Both were to act as their servants for an unspecified length of time. Contracts of this sort are often negotiated with these barbarians. Chong

112

agreed. He forthwith turned as docile and submissive as ever.

"But have you thought of the trick he could have played on them? It struck every one of us at this stage of the interrogation. Do you know that at the sight of the bottle all the men had brought out their drinking mugs? If, instead of persisting in a stupid show of force which could logically only end to his disadvantage, he had pretended to comply with good grace to their demands, he could then have given each a tot of this liquid they had mistaken for alcohol. He would thus have been rid of his assailants then and there. Better still, he would have found himself in possession of the two mules they had, not to mention their burden and any amount of provisions. He would never have had to account for his action. The law is not so rigid in those mountains as in our civilized districts. The police there have little power and it was a case of legitimate self-defense.

"The whole of China would have applauded such an ingenious maneuver. Do you realize that even in their pitiful condition they had a fortune in their hands? A mere flick of the wrist, and they could have come back to our province as wealthy travelers and not as tattered beggars. Chong's family and all the notables of Yi-Ping would have welcomed them with open arms. Furthermore, they would have brought back with them a delightful story that would have met with universal admiration. . . . But no, sir. They thought more highly of this benighted potion than of fame and fortune, their own lives, or saving

113

face. They disdained this windfall. They let the opportunity slip through their fingers and preferred an
arrangement whereby they both became slaves."

"Incredible stupidity," I said.

"That's what we thought, sir. Incredible stupidity,
or else criminal folly that annihilates every other sentiment, including the instinct of self-preservation.

"So they started working for their masters. The
latter employed them on the foulest tasks and
treated them worse than their mules. They dragged
them along with them on long nocturnal expedi-
tions and made them carry heavy burdens. On reach-
ing a halting place, they had to prepare the camp,
look after the animals, and cook the food before
being allowed to rest. That was what their life was
like. They accepted everything: the most repulsive
chores, insults, and blows. They were intractable only
on one point, sir—the bottle. Listen to these words
of Chong's. They illustrate his diseased mind rather
well:

" 'At nighttime, Mandarin President, we had
trained ourselves to sleep by turns, and whichever
of us was on watch used to guard the bottle. Our precautions were not superfluous, for it had incited the
rapacity of some of the men. They were intrigued
by our stubborn attitude about it and by the care we
took to keep it safe.

" 'I was worried to realize that a sort of legend
was taking shape around it. They began to look upon
it as something endowed with mysterious powers. Often, in the evening, they would gather in a group not

114

far from us and talk in whispers, pointing at us with their fingers. I tried to catch the drift of their conversation; it was difficult, for among themselves they spoke a language different from ours. But they all believed, I know, that the bottle contained a magic elixir, the possession of which would bring them great wealth.

"'After the first month of our captivity, almost every night shadowy forms kept prowling around us in the hope of catching us both asleep. We would talk in a loud voice and generally that was enough to scare them off; but on one occasion, Mandarin President, I had to fight with one of them who decided to rob us. He was stronger than I. I was about to succumb; but while he held me by the throat, bearing down on me with his full weight, my wife bit him so violently that he gave a yell of pain and woke up all the others. The brigand chief came up to us. He was a man of honor. He flew into a rage and upbraided his men. He ordered them to abide by the terms of the contract. Thus we miraculously kept our property.'

"In fact, sir, according to the disjointed explanations which Chong added to his statement, it seemed to us that the chief, too, had come to look upon this mysterious liquid as a talisman. You see the suggestion of magic cropping up again? It was impossible to escape. The frenzy that took possession of the usually calm prisoner, whenever they tried to lay a finger on the bottle, would account for this sentiment in superstitious barbarians. The brigand chief may have

115

feared neither god nor devil, but the colorless liquid no doubt suggested nothing good to his mind. As a responsible leader, he had to be on his guard against the vengeance of the jinns of the mountains if his men happened to get hold of it by means of a ruse contrary to the agreement. That's about the only rational explanation for his attitude, which Chong regarded as a miraculous intervention. Whatever the reasons, he made his authority felt and the treasure remained out of danger from then on.

"Chong and his wife spent several months with the brigands—three or four months, he could not tell exactly how long. He appeared to regard this captivity in retrospect as a period that was not too bad on the whole. When the attempts to rob them ceased, he told us, they had been less unhappy than in the town in which they had lived before. The brigands always had enough to eat and their leftovers provided abundant meals. Some of his statements even tend to suggest that he was not far from regarding their capture as an occasion for rejoicing:

" 'During this period, Mandarin President, we had hardly a care in the world and we ate regularly every day. We put on weight and recovered our strength. We adapted ourselves to the harsh conditions of the mountains and to physical fatigue. My wife even trained herself to clamber up the steep slopes un- aided, feeling her way along with a stick. Without this apprenticeship we should have been unable to surmount the ordeals in store for us during the rest of our journey. We were well aware of this, and that's

116

why we made no attempt at an earlier escape. Later on we felt that those brigands had been a godsend. But for them we should never have been strong enough to reach the province of Li-Kang, and I should have been prevented from accomplishing my mission. . . .'

"He occasionally spoke like this, sir, in a state of almost religious ecstasy. He used the word 'mission' to describe the dreadful task he had taken upon himself when he was raving one evening; and the hardships he endured throughout the journey he frequently referred to as 'tests.' There was a strange gleam in his eye when he uttered these words, a gleam that was like—this is monstrous, but I have to admit it—like the gleam you see in the eyes of our saintly hermits when the hour of annihilation approaches as a reward for a virtuous life. I can picture them both at nighttime, under the stars, dreaming of this mission and impatiently waiting to recover strength enough to accomplish it!

"When they felt they were sufficiently fit, and having acquired a fairly thorough knowledge of the mountains, they resumed their march toward the north. They succeeded in escaping. They seized the opportunity one evening when the brigands were all drunk, and sneaked out of the camp without being observed. They took nothing with them but a few provisions and, needless to say, the bottle.

"They trudged all that night and all the following day, wishing to escape any possible pursuit. Actually, judging by his description of the brigands and by

117

the fatalism that is generally found among adventurers of that sort, I feel sure they did not bother to run after them. Perhaps the chief was even happy to be rid of them and their talisman, which caused discontent among his band. But they dared not risk a further postponement. Toward evening, after scaling a pass, they reached an inhabited valley. Only then did they halt, exhausted but delighted, as he told us in that incongruous language of his, at having triumphantly passed this initial 'test.' "

FOURTEEN

"They started off again first thing in the morning.
They spent no time in the valley, which was an oasis
in this mountainous desert. They did not want to lose
a moment. They made their way instinctively toward
the north, as though the pole of their monstrous desire had inscribed invisible magnetic lines for them
through the chaos of ravines and defiles.

"It was yet another folly: they were thus drawn
toward the highest peaks of the range running down
from Tibet, toward the passes the caravans avoid,
which only an occasional smuggler uses and which
are snowbound most of the winter. But the usual

119

route for travelers meant a detour of several hundred li. Their impatience would not accept it. Chong claimed to have weighed all the difficulties and to have then decided to forge straight ahead, firm in the belief that heaven would not abandon them.

"The most extraordinary part of the story, sir, is that they succeeded. I don't know those mountains, but from accounts of the few explorers who have been there they are enough to make one shiver with fright and they have a bad name in the whole of southern China. Above a certain altitude the paths peter out and one can only move forward by following the river beds. Still higher, one is above the level of the forests and one finds oneself lost in a wilderness of jagged rocks, the very sight of which inspires terror. The climate is unhealthy. The sun hardly ever appears. Gray clouds and pernicious mists hover perpetually over the slopes, seeping into any living creature that ventures there and rotting the sparse vegetation."

"It's a description of hell you're giving me, venerable sir."

"At all events, a not very hospitable country, sir. Yet they clambered up those slopes bristling with obstacles. And they lived up there for several months, eating wild plants and repulsive animals. How did that sickly, blind woman manage to get across those ridges? And, on top of it all, she had a relapse. She started coughing and gasping for breath as soon as they reached the level of the mists. That climate and the strain were obviously anything but beneficial. He was soon obliged to support her, to drag her along, and sometimes even carry her when she was completely out of breath.

"She showed great courage, he told us. We can well believe him on that score, as well as when he described his own hardships and suffering, proudly asserting that they had both gone beyond the limits of human endurance. He had sworn to tell the truth, and we must give him his due: no one detected a single falsehood in his statement. All the evidence goes to show that in crossing those mountains under such conditions they accomplished a feat that surpasses imagination."

The old Chinese fell silent and contemplated his chopsticks lying like two parallel bars on the tablecloth. He seemed to be harassed once again by one of those profound thoughts of his. It contracted his muscles and expanded his cheeks. He leaned over toward me. His physical tension manifested itself in a number of sententious remarks, to which I listened with as much curiosity as to his story.

"If those two creatures, sir, had been impelled by the spirit of *Good* instead of being possessed by a demon, they would have been capable of accomplishing the most sublime feats—I'd stake my life on that, as the saying goes. If only they had performed the same actions under the impulse of a noble ideal, all the inhabitants of China would have glorified them as heroes or as saints, so strongly do exploits of this sort appeal to the masses in my country.

121

"How they had managed to deploy such energy, such tenacity, such courage even, it must be admitted, with such an ignoble aim in view, constitutes a problem of a philosophical order which is liable to give rise to disturbing reflections. While listening to the account of this arduous, tragic odyssey—an odyssey that, by virtue of certain signs of devotion, was occasionally admirable in itself—the whole court was plunged into a state of intense stupefaction that left no room for any other sentiment. Like our greatest sages, I also tried to throw some light on this case by applying my knowledge of the human species to it, and also my experience of disease. I could not discover a single satisfactory solution. I find it hard to accept as true that the spirit of Evil alone could have dictated this heroic conduct. I find myself sometimes dreaming that there was some other incentive—a motive?—the motive Chong had never been able to reveal and which perhaps lay buried in the innermost depths of his subconscious."

"Stop worrying about it, venerable sir," I told him. "You're cudgeling your brains to no purpose. If there is some obscure point in all this, neither you nor I will ever clear it up when the Supreme Court of Yi-Ping with its wise magistrates and notables was incapable of doing so. It would be presumptuous of us to try to tackle this enigma. Please go on."

"I shall only describe their crossing of the final pass, the highest of all, and above all what happened to them shortly afterward, for it is remarkable.

"For several months they had been walking, stumbling, dragging themselves along, striving despite their suffering to climb higher every day, drawing closer every minute to that pass which opened the road toward the Promised Land. For several weeks they had not seen a soul, and what food supplies they had, patiently hoarded with this hazardous crossing in mind, were quickly running out. At night-time they slept huddled close together in a fissure of the rocks.

"They managed at last to reach the pass before winter, before the great cold and the snow, and started descending the farther slope. But they were in such poor condition that they soon had to stop. They had gone, as they put it, beyond the limits of their endurance, and the woman's disease had flared up again. She was half dead, he told us. Here are his very words:

" 'A pernicious mist had penetrated her lungs and was devouring them, Mandarin President. She could no longer move. She sank down at the foot of a rock. She mumbled a few words. By placing my ear against her mouth I understood that she was begging me to abandon her and go on without her to the province of Li-Kang to fulfill my mission there. I refused to do this. I felt we were both engaged on this mission and that I needed her to bring it to a successful conclusion. The cold suddenly swept over us, for this slope was not protected from the winds. Night was falling. The first flakes of snow thickened the mist. We could not go on, yet a lengthy halt meant death. I thought we were going to perish there and, just as I was beginning to give way to sheer despair, Mandarin President, I had proof that heaven had not abandoned us.'

"Heaven again, sir, you observe. He had adopted this sacrilegious mode of expression once and for all.

" 'I lay down beside her so as to afford her some shelter. A gust of wind pierced a gap in the fog. I noticed thirty yards below us the outline of a roof. This apparition was so extraordinary in this wilderness that I thought I was raving, suffering from an hallucination caused by overstrain and the approach of death.'

"He took great pains to describe the fantastic nature of this apparition. Depending on the swirling mist, it was sometimes buried in deep snow and sometimes it emerged like a ghost through a thin, transparent curtain. His idea of a mirage was understandable. The blind woman could be of no help to him. He rubbed his watering eyes until he was convinced that his mind was not wandering.

"There was a hut there, no doubt long abandoned, but still in fairly good condition, set into a mass of rocks that protected it from the storms. Smugglers had probably built this refuge at some time or other to serve them as a halting place in the days when the illicit traffic between the provinces was at its highest pitch. The roof, made of rough branches, was half rotten but still kept out the rain and snow, except for a few leaks. The walls, of the same material, afforded reasonable shelter. A fireplace had been erected in the middle—a raised patch of trampled earth, like those in our country cottages. In one corner there was an ample store of dry wood. It was a providential asylum, and some excuse can be found for Chong's state of mind when he still believed it was a miracle even after recognizing the reality of his vision.

"He had great difficulty in struggling to his feet and carrying his companion to this refuge. He laid her down on the floor, where she collapsed, unconscious. He tried to light a fire and only succeeded after several attempts. He was trembling from head to foot. He heated some water. He managed to make the sick woman swallow a few mouthfuls of the brew which for many unfortunates takes the place of tea. He could do nothing more for her. He sat motionless in front of the fire, contemplating this wretched creature who, from all appearances, had no more than a few hours to live."

"A sad vigil, venerable sir," I said.

"Extremely sad, sir. He gave us a heart-rending account of it. Night had fallen. Outside, a storm had broken. The room, lit only by the fire, was gradually invaded by thick smoke. There are no chimneys in these huts. Drops of icy water kept dripping over them at irregular intervals. The woman, her features drawn and her limbs contracted, gave no sign of life except when she was occasionally racked by violent fits of shivering. As for him, he remained crouching by the hearth, too exhausted to sleep. He too began to feel the first effects of fever. His teeth started chattering. He was suffering from all the fatigue accumulated during the past months. His eyes wandered from the prostrate form by his side to a corner of the hut where he had wedged the bottle between two logs. . . . What thoughts must have run through his head in this tragic situation, between this dying companion of his and this devil's potion, at a time when he was on the verge of collapse himself, knowing he was in a benighted region far from all habitation and that they had hardly any food left? He was not able to enlighten us on this point. He claimed that the fever had dimmed his memory.

"For he was the one who fell seriously ill in the end. And the woman did not die. On the contrary, she soon recovered, as you'll see presently. . . . Those disinherited, sickly and decrepit souls, sir, whose life seems to hang on a thread, always manage to find in the innermost depths of their unworthy carcasses resources which paradoxically prolong the period of their outrageous incarnation on this earth, whereas sturdy, healthy people are carried off by the slightest infection. I've often observed that."

"Such, venerable sir, is the absurdity of this world."

"As you say, sir, and we can do nothing about it. . . . Anyway, she recovered, and rapidly. The next day he felt weaker and weaker and did not move from his position except to rekindle the fire and put some water on to boil. She sat up all of a sudden. Color returned to her cheeks. She spoke in her normal voice. He realized she was alive and felt, he told us, an intense joy. But at that very moment he was felled by his illness and lapsed into unconsciousness."

"This journey is certainly no pleasure trip," I said.

"I warned you, sir. They spent some grim days up there, it can't be denied. I can understand how you feel. While listening to Chong's account of his misfortunes, we too experienced a similar sensation. The cruelty of the Chinese is, as I told you before, a mere legend. We are capable of being moved by human suffering as much as any other race. In the present case, I give you my word, we really had to reason with ourselves, to remind ourselves of Chong's villainy and the aim he had in mind, not to let ourselves be carried away by undeserved compassion."

"I'm having to make that effort of memory myself. But will this tragic situation soon come to an end?"

"It will become still more tragic, sir. For in this refuge which they had looked upon as a gift from God, they presently endured a ghastly torment, more terrible than sickness and want. I could skip this incident if your sensibilities. . . ."

"Hypocrite, tell me about this torment! I can't imagine anything worse happening to them. What is this fresh atrocity?"

"The rats, sir. A frightful scourge in certain provinces of China."

FIFTEEN

"Rats, sir," he went on, "are a plague in China, and in that hut they had no protection against them. They slept on the bare floor, without bedclothes, and the wood fire was their only source of light.

"The day after they arrived, while he was watching over his companion, a lone rat put in a furtive appearance. Half its stiffened body emerged into the room through the branches when Chong, who was dozing, caught sight of it.

" 'It didn't make a sound,' he told us, 'it didn't move an inch.'

"His glance had fallen at random on this inquisitive snout. He had the sensation that the rat had

123

been there for some time, for several hours, peering, listening, sniffing, spying with all its faculties on the new inhabitants of the hut. He was overwhelmed by a superstitious terror, paralyzing him for a moment. He more or less told us that this vermin appeared to him like a demon bent on mischief and deliberately sent by hell to foil his scheme!

"Chong's mind, mark you, was populated by phantoms. He was instinctively inclined to attribute an occult significance to the most trivial natural manifestations. It's true that excessive suffering and privation might have affected his brain. I can easily imagine his being fascinated by that rat, fancying he saw in it the incarnation of some malevolent power. And this illusion persisted.

"In the end, however, he shifted his position. The rat at once disappeared as discreetly as it had arrived. It did not show itself again that day, neither it nor any other like it, and the night went by without further alarm. Only the following evening the rats appeared in vast numbers. At that time Chong was prostrate on the floor, in the throes of fever. It was the blind woman, sir—the blind woman who had miraculously come back to life, who with her unsteady hands had succeeded him in kindling the fire—it was she who withstood the assaults and, in the darkness in which she lived, fiercely defended their few mouthfuls of food and the flesh and blood of their bodies; for these animals are ferocious.

"When he was not completely unconscious, delirium made him confuse these beasts with the chimeras of some other world. So the account he gave us of these battles was somewhat disjointed. As you can imagine, the sight must have made a deep impression on someone in the throes of fever. I've noted certain passages which are nevertheless of interest:

"'The demons made their infernal power felt shortly after dusk, Mandarin President. I can remember only some of those nights. I've lost all recollection of the others.

"'I was lying by the fire, shivering the whole time in spite of the heat, my body as heavy as lead. It began with some strange noises above our heads. They came from the thick layer of decaying twigs that formed the roof; they sounded like the whispering of malevolent spirits preparing a foul scheme in the dark. My heart turned to stone. I saw my wife's face stiffen. She was gripping her stick, standing stock still, her body leaning forward, trying desperately to sniff out the direction of the threat. But our enemies formed an unbroken line. The whole roof heaved and creaked, as though infused with a life of its own. The din grew progressively louder. Some sharp little cries, betraying hideous delight, made me quake with fear, as a ghostly chuckle might have done. I, I who had my sight, could soon discern more and more numerous, more and more aggressive undulations that swept over the walls of the room and vanished into the shadows. I knew they were creeping down and closing in on us. My wife did not move. I made a desperate effort to raise myself up on one elbow and explore the floor around us, in terror of finding one of the monsters there and certain they would soon all be there. She sensed my fear. Feeling her way, she threw more logs on the fire.

" 'The attack was not slow in coming. As always, it took me aback. As always, it occurred in an unforeseen manner. Sometimes quite close, in the full light of the flames, at other times brushing my limbs as I struggled to peer into the farthest shadows, one of these creatures would rise up, its pointed snout motionless, its cruel red eyes fixed on us as on a sure prey. Once again it had escaped my notice. Invisibly, as though by magic, it had crossed the illuminated patch.

" 'I gave a groan. My arms felt so heavy that I could not lift a finger in defense. The rat jumped aside. It mocked me with a somersault and vanished into the shadows. My wife had heard and understood. She turned her head carefully in the direction of the horde and started laying about her with her stick, which resounded on the hard floor. At the very moment she put the first beast to flight, I noticed another behind her. It had come up as silently as its predecessor and was spying on us with the same patient and relentless air. I shouted to put her on her guard. She came back, sweeping the ground all around her. At this stage a rustling sound warned us that a whole army had imperceptibly advanced. Leaps and grotesque somersaults announced a general movement of withdrawal, a retreat exactly sufficient to put them out of range of the blows delivered

131

at random. . . . There was method in these maneuvers. They knew quite well that she could not see them and that I was paralyzed! They withdrew—a few paces at the most. They formed a circle barely larger than the illuminated area. I could make out constellations of red pinpoints scrutinizing the clumsy hand that wielded the pathetic weapon. When a flame rose a little higher than the others it cast terrifying shadows on the ground.

" 'I saw enormous creatures, bigger than cats, more horrible than dragons, all animated by the insatiable thirst to do harm. They were *intelligent,* Mandarin President—intelligent, perverse, and well-organized. Their assaults were synchronized. They relieved one another, battalion by battalion, so as to allow us no respite. They tried to overwhelm us by presenting themselves in the most grisly forms their genius could devise. Their very appearance sometimes brought a cry of terror to my lips, and the diabolical cunning of their countless manifestations foiled my wife's guard. She got up. She made the rounds of the room, feeling her way about, tapping on the roof, the walls, the floor. The brisk ebb and flow of the reserves lying in wait in the filth prolonged the sound of the blows. The whole hut was haunted by spirits bent on our destruction. She had not finished her rounds before others had already crept into the middle of the room, mocking her erratic thrusts. They laughed at her infirmity like wicked children. Repulsive swarms brushed against my legs. My shudders scarcely drove them off. The blind woman came back, not daring to strike any longer for fear of hitting me. Her anxious hands felt my body. She clung to me. She confined herself to brandishing her stick in all directions, while I informed her whenever I could of the most immediate danger. We could only think of protecting a minute area around us.

" 'Then they embarked relentlessly on a harassing series of forward thrusts and withdrawals. Sometimes, when my companion's arm grew tired, when she no longer had sufficient resource to vary the intensity and extent of her blows, when the monotony of her efforts increased their audacity, the circle of seething flesh closed in so far as to engulf us, like the hands of a strangler with a thousand fingers. Sometimes the vise loosened a bit, when she summoned up her strength and when one of the demons, struck by chance, did a somersault and gave a sharp cry which sowed momentary alarm among the serried ranks. But order was quickly restored, under the effect of a stubborn persistence, of a superior authority. The monsters would then launch themselves at us again.

" 'I can't remember how many nights my wife spent like this. I frequently lost consciousness, my head buried in my arms. Can you imagine her then, Mandarin President, alone, facing this accursed army in the dark?

" 'She could tell from my silence and my posture that I had closed my eyes and was of no more help to her. She redoubled her vigilance, went out of her way to make up for the handicap of her infirmity by the sharpness of her ear, by that sense of danger which

133

blind people possess, and by *reflection,* Mandarin President. . . .

"'It was, as I am aware I said before, a battle of wits. She concentrated all her faculties on varying, in a thousand different ways, the extent, speed, and threatening impression of her blows. She racked her brains at every moment to invent an original stratagem in her series of gestures, an unusual tone in her shouts. Each discovery of this sort, by narrowing the field of innovations, made the next one all the harder. Our lives depended on the strength and speed of her imagination. At every moment her mind had to assemble the elements of an effect of surprise, for rats soon grow accustomed to anything. She had to surpass them in cunning, outwit them by giving them an impression of unflagging watchfulness and keen sight. She confessed to me later that her efforts resulted in a torture that was harder to bear than the physical strain.

"'If she relaxed her vigilance for a second, as sometimes happened, we would wake up covered with these foul animals which chewed up our clothing and nibbled our very flesh. One night, I remember, Mandarin President, I had succumbed to one of my torpors. I had a dreadful nightmare. I dreamt that a legion of dragons had entered my chest and were eating out my heart. I suffered this horror for a very long time, paralyzed by disgust and pain. When I managed at last to sit up and give a yell which woke me, the rats burst out from everywhere. I felt as though a flock of these demons were emerging from my body and scattering in all directions, screaming with rage. My hair stood on end; my blood ran cold. My eyes fell on the figure of my wife outlined against the flames, and something about the shape of this sleeping form increased my horror without my being able to understand the reason. When at last I dared to lift my head and look more closely, I saw one of those ghastly animals clinging to her forehead, fastening onto her skin, hanging on to her with all the strength of its claws. It had planted its fangs into the wretched woman's nose and its snout was quivering, drenched in blood. She did not move. She had succumbed to her exhaustion and I was scarcely strong enough to groan. Without letting go of its prey, the demon darted a glance at me with its red eyes. It remained so for a long time, threatening me, until my wife eventually reacted to the pain by bringing both her hands up to her forehead in a reflex of distress.' "

"Stop!" I broke in. "My own blood is running cold as well. That's what you wanted, I can see. Well, you've succeeded. But that's enough."

"All I've done is translate Chong's own words for you, sir. He seemed anxious to let us know all the details of his tragic situation. And I don't think you realize yet the exact nature of the peril that was threatening them, at least from his point of view."

"It seems quite clear to me. They were in danger of being eaten alive."

"That goes without saying, sir, just as they were in danger of dying of hunger; for what remained of their provisions excited the greed of the vermin to the point of madness. Even though the woman carried their meager larder on her, the rats had succeeded in breaking into it. Yet, incredible though it may seem, that was not the real cause of their anguish."

"I don't understand, venerable sir."

"Because, despite the facts, you persist in endowing him with your own reasoning, your own instincts, which are those of a normal human being. It was only little by little, through his feverish insistence, that we ourselves finally came to understand the true nature of his horror.

"In his rare moments of lucidity, sir, he was frightened of yielding to temptation!"

"What temptation?"

"He was afraid the agony might become unbearable. He dreaded it might reach such a degree of intensity that they might go out of their minds. He was terrified at the thought that in a moment of weakness he might dispatch his assailants with the precious contents of the bottle which had so far been preserved intact, in spite of all the hazards."

"The poison," I muttered. "That's true. I never thought of that."

"You would have thought of it if you had been in their predicament. This torture, the mere account of which filled you with horror—do you imagine you would have endured it for over a week? Make a sum total of the suffering represented by fever, sleeplessness, rat bites, disgust, horror, and fear of starvation. Now remember that, as during their meeting with the robbers, they had an easy way of destroying their foes. You'll agree then, I'm sure, that it needed superhuman will power—outrageous will power, certainly, but nevertheless heroic—not to make use of this method.

"A handful of rice steeped in the potion would have been enough to poison a dozen rats perhaps. With the bodies cut up and sprinkled anew, they had the means at their disposal of destroying the whole cursed brood in a single night. These animals feed on one another. This would have assured them sleep and rest, and at the same time an almost inexhaustible supply of fresh food, since they knew how to prepare it so as to render the poison harmless."

"I can understand the temptation. And they did not yield to it?"

"Not a drop, sir!"

"I admit, that argues a sort of heroism."

"It was above all when he thought of the possibility of giving in that his mind in an absurd manner identified the rats with the creatures of some unknown hell. This became clear after his many explanations. It's a curious sign of his disconcerting mentality. He regarded these beasts as the instruments of some malevolent jinn who had tried to exploit their instinct and make them succumb to this

137

temptation. By analyzing this psychological complex, an expert might, I fancy, discern a hint of method in his madness, in the absence of all logic."

"No psychology, no analysis, venerable sir—you promised me. Only the facts."

"These are the facts, sir," said the old Chinese with sudden animation.

"He told us with shame that he had almost admitted defeat. It happened the day he had the vision of the rat devouring his companion's face. At that moment, he told us, he had a moment of despair. He managed to drag himself as far as the corner where their priceless treasure stood. He took out the plug which served as a cork. His suffering was too inhuman. He was about to prepare the liberating bait by sacrificing a little of this fabulous elixir.

"And it was his wife who held him back, sir! She had heard the noise and guessed his intention. She restrained his arm. She placed her sightless face in front of his with such a painful air of reproach that he blushed and felt ashamed of himself. . . . I can't control my feelings when I think of their behavior. Which of these two was the madder, sir, can you tell me? She, by opposing the only reasonable act he could still accomplish? Or he—he, who felt gratitude and almost religious admiration for this creature? He, of whom it was impossible to tell whether his veneration was due to the tireless devotion of this lunatic or to the gesture which condemned them both to torture?"

138

The old Chinese fidgeted on his bench and went on passionately:

"Here are more facts. She promised him, the better to persuade him, that she would not let herself fall asleep any more. He in his turn promised not to repeat his attempt. And both of them together swore that under no condition would they draw off a single drop of this poison. You may well wonder at the oath whereby they undertook to oppose each other if either of them showed the least sign of relenting.

"They recorked the bottle. And then, sir, at that precise moment, he solemnly assured us, he felt much better! According to him, his recovery had begun at that very second. Naturally he saw in this yet another miracle.

"They both observed the terms of this outrageous pact. And when one of them felt himself weakening, do you know what the other did, sir? Here are still more facts! The more resolute one at the moment, the one on whom the role of savior devolved, would take the bottle and place it silently in his companion's lap—as though it were a sovereign remedy against weakening, one of those relics which sick people are made to touch! And the other would always be grateful for this gesture. He felt the profound significance of it, his courage would return. And, both shedding tears of joy, they would then in turn place a cheek against the icy glass! Two maniacs, sir, two maniacs—there's no other possible description for them, and I myself am mad to think of any

139

other! Two maniacs, that's it—two creatures beyond the confines of our world, whose perverse instincts had been monstrously developed by hardship to such a pitch as to eliminate all sentiment, all desire, all human reaction, to the exclusive benefit of a morbid passion!"

SIXTEEN

"Compose yourself, venerable sir," I said. "Calm down, I beseech you, for your indignation is contagious and I feel that I too am going to lose my self-control. I agree with you, it's a waste of time to try to find a reason for acts of madness. But it's also childish to get irritated because you can't find any. You're the one behaving now like a child. Pull yourself together and calmly continue with your account of the facts."

"You're perfectly right, sir. I must ask you to forgive me.

"The rat episode comes to an end with Chong's recovery. He was soon able to get up and share the watch with his wife, and even kill a few of the beasts with his stick. So they had enough to eat and after a few days were sufficiently strong to set off again. And their journey continued. They crossed the highest mountains. They encountered other obstacles, all of much the same sort. I don't think they could be of any great interest to you."

"I've formed a pretty clear picture of that trek, venerable sir, and of the spirit that inspired it. Besides, didn't you warn me that from beginning to end it was a repetition of similar incidents whose philosophical essence can be summed up in a very few words?"

"Yes, sir: hardship, thirst, fatigue, and fear—in short, suffering."

"Tests, as Chong put it?"

"Tests. That was the very word he used."

"The sources of hostility being still, I suppose, men, nature, and beasts?"

"That's a rather peculiar way of regarding the events, but up to a point it's correct."

"Tests from which they always emerged victorious?"

"Always sir—by some unheard-of chance and as though they were protected by some occult power."

"That's all I wanted to know, venerable sir. Go on with the rest of the journey."

"It takes us more or less up to the end of the accused's statement of evidence. The rest you know, or can easily imagine. They reached Yi-Ping in the state I've already described. He resumed his job as assistant executioner under his father. He now proved to be as conscientious and skillful as he had once been careless and clumsy; he was eager, he had vowed, to become a chief executioner. His diligence reaped its reward. His touch became so masterful that shortly afterward, on his father's death, the high mandarins of the province overlooked his bad behavior in the past and entrusted him with these functions.

"Then he embarked methodically on his series of crimes, following the plan he had drawn up. The hideous stage-setting was perfectly adapted to it. In the absence of the other officials it was easy for him to keep his assistants at a distance and to pour out the poison. In the shadows he would watch the arrival of the condemned man. He would observe each of his gestures. As soon as the condemned man had gulped down the glass of whiskey, Chong the executioner would step forward into the full light in his ceremonial garb. His victim's collapse was attributed to emotional shock. He operated in this manner seven times in three years.

"It now remains for me to tell you about the rest of the trial: in fact, the trial proper, all that I've dealt with so far being only the preliminary investigation . . . that is, if you're still willing to hear it, of course."

"If I'm still willing, venerable sir? I shan't close an eye, I shan't rest a moment until I've heard the charges put forward by the prosecution and the arguments of the defense."

"You shall hear them, sir, but not until tomorrow.

143

I'm sorry to cause you a sleepless night, but I've talked too much this evening and my mind is becoming confused."

I left the city of Yin-Yang in a state of intense excitement. As soon as I was outside the ancient town walls I noticed a white form laying by the side of the road. From it arose a sound of lamentation.

It was my guardian angel. His plumes were damp from the bitter tears he had shed while waiting for me.

"I heard everything," he said. *"Animus meminisse horret.* I forced myself to listen out of love for you— an extremely laudable effort on my part. I am pained and distressed to see you lending an ear to the inanities of that old Chinese. His two heroes are perverse and absurd creatures, he admits it himself—criminal lunatics whose behavior is an outrage to reason and moral sense."

"So you, too, are appalled by the behavior of that fellow Chong!" I sorrowfully observed. "You too, like that old Chinese."

"Well, yes. . . . His raving is the only worthwhile element in the whole story. But why expatiate on foul, ignoble acts that everyone condemns? And you, you whose brain is still malleable, you feast on these absurd adventures in which I have searched in vain for a spark of humanity.

"Ah, come back! Come back with me, I beseech you! I'll lend you new books, and you'll at last be able to write a real story. I've prepared a long list of works in which you'll find the nourishment best suited to your youth. You'll choose your characters out of them yourself. You'll write a story glorifying mother love, or paternal love, or filial love, or conjugal love, or platonic love, or adulterous love, or incestuous love, or bestial love if you must, but anyway a story containing a little human warmth."

With my mind in a whirl, I drew away from Yin-Yang and returned with him to the world of moderation.

And next day, shortly before dusk, I made my way back once more towards the magical city. And my guardian angel, my faithful guardian angel, kept me company all the way. And the litany of his advice, his warnings, his entreaties, accompanied my every step. And I, in my ingratitude, was insensible to this devotion!

I now feel a flush of shame mounting to my cheeks as I make this confession, but—and I give you my word, this is strictly true—I was beginning to find him slightly importunate. His solicitude appeared hypocritical to me and I found his persistent attempts to impose his exclusive paradise on me tactless. As he begged me for the thousandth time to undergo a cure of disintoxication and to seek asylum in the human species, I had the temerity to reply:

"Now listen, Guardian Angel. I haven't your experience, but I've traveled quite a bit and met all sorts of people. I don't speak the sacred languages, though I've glanced through a few rose-colored pages; but when it comes to Chinese customs, my knowledge must be almost equal to your own. After all, what are your qualifications for coming down to earth and talking to me about humanity?"

"My qualifications? I've a hundred thousand of them."

"A hundred thousand?" I said.

"I've read a hundred thousand books," he declared impressively.

"A hundred thousand books!"

"A hundred thousand books," he repeated, ruffling his feathers. "Ever since I was born, you realize, I've lived in a corner of Paradise. I've furnished it to my taste, and no one comes and disturbs me there. I've blocked up all the entrances. While you were traveling and meeting all sorts of people, I, I'll have you know, forbade myself all distraction. I didn't once put my nose out of doors. I kept myself pure. I fiercely avoided every contact, apart from Letters. I guarded myself jealously against every influence outside my cell that might have hindered my intellectual concentration and interfered with the life—that seething, swarming, sparkling, tumultuous life—which throbs in the twenty million or so lines that have been written and read.

"My qualifications? My qualifications for talking to you about humanity? Listen to this. I own a vast filing cabinet filled to bursting point with slips of paper: slips of paper arranged in alphabetical order. And on these slips everything, absolutely *everything* of interest to man, is written down, do you hear?—all

146

the thoughts, all the feelings, all the wisdom, all the manias, all the intelligence, all the emotions, all the furies, all the uncertainties, all the errors, all the terrors, all the virtues, all the vices, all the *passions* of literature! And you ask me on what authority I speak to you about humanity!"

"Oh, all right," I said impatiently. "Now I'm going to tell you a parable, Guardian Angel."

"Don't use a word when you don't know what it means," he replied, shrugging his wings.

"An allegory, if you prefer. It's about a friend of mine. His father, who was the watchman of a vast building where some pianos were stored, began bringing the son with him to this place at a very tender age. He therefore learned to walk among pianos. These were soon familiar objects to him, which his childish imagination endowed with a mind of their own. Crawling about on all fours, he discovered the pedals, the legs and, a little later on, the smooth wooden sides which his fingers stroked lovingly.

"His knowledge of pianos gradually became more and more complete. One day, by stretching up on tiptoe, he managed to raise the lid of a keyboard an inch or two. Peering with delight, as though in a dream, at the fantastic tile pattern of the black and white keys, he had a revelation of beauty. His heart was filled with joy. He often repeated this gesture, without ever daring to lay a finger on the ivories—what delighted him was the majestic calm and silence of these motionless objects.

"His experience soon embraced the piano stools,

147

whose slow gyrations were a source of infinite ecstasy to him. He went on growing and, after a few years, had a fresh view of the instruments. He contemplated the top of them, and the great shining surfaces of the grand pianos awakened a poetic instinct in him.

"When his father died, he was given the job of watchman. He went on living among the pianos, enriching his knowledge at every instant by an original angle or unexpected molding. Frequently, as in the days of his infancy, he would furtively raise a lid to peer at the keyboard with a smile of satisfaction, just as overawed as ever by its cold pure geometry and mysterious silence.

"He lived to a very advanced age, after seeing thousands and thousands of pianos of every size and model pass through the building, for they were frequently changed. No one in the world had an experience of pianos comparable to his.

"Well, believe it or not, Guardian Angel, at his death he still did not know how to play a piano. He could not even read a note of music."

"What happened then?" my guardian angel asked.

"That's the end of the story," I said.

"Just another of your stories without head or tail to it. You're trying to lull me to sleep and make me relax my vigilance, for we've now arrived outside the accursed place. Don't go in."

The ramparts of Yin-Yang rose before us. He placed himself in front of me, unfurling his wings. I tried to reason with him.

"Now listen, Guardian Angel. Let's make a pact. Grant me a few more escapades and one day, when I have more experience, I'll write a story for you, I promise—a story for you alone, one of those stories for which you have established the norm and restricted the scope. It will fit automatically into one of your compartments, under one of your headings— under Thrillers or Psychological Novels, under Novelettes, Tales, or plain Accounts, but it won't be betwixt and between. There will be nothing Chinese about the characters. As in real life, they'll act or they'll think, but they won't do both. They will be tender-hearted or harsh, sad or gay, logical or absurd, but I vow they won't be monsters beyond the confines of humanity who weep after having just laughed. . . . Nothing but the probable, nothing but the human, I swear. Heavens, I can see it, I can feel this future work already! You think I'm incapable of writing it? How little you know me! Have confidence in me, Guardian Angel. I can already reveal the subject of it to you; it will be the story of a tormented heart that seeks its way without finding it, and finally despairs. What do you think of that? It will reveal such secrets that anyone will be able to say: 'That's the sensation I had the other day while drinking my coffee.' You'll conclude: 'There's nothing new under the sun,' and, in speaking of me, 'I always said he had it in him.'

"But in the meantime don't be selfish. Let me go in."

"You shan't go in," he said.

I had come in vain to the limit of every possible self-sacrifice. He had not listened to me. His attitude had become threatening. His voice grated like that of an evil angel. I was frightened. . . .

Ah, what more could I say to excuse my conduct? Had I lost all self-possession? Had the fumes emanating from the city of Yin-Yang disturbed my brain? I took a step forward and bumped against him rather violently. He did not budge. I saw his great wings slowly folding back.

I fought. We struggled. He was the stronger. Inexorably the wings closed around me. In a defensive reaction I clutched hold of them and tried to force them apart. The feathers came away in my hand. I was astonished to see that they were as hard and pointed as daggers. I lost my head. I seized one of them and struck out. A jet of blood spurted. His grip weakened and he slowly collapsed.

I took to my heels without daring to look back. I had acted, certainly, in a state of legitimate self-defense—he might have strangled me on the spot to save my soul!—but I was alarmed all the same. As I entered the forbidden city, I trembled as I heard a dying voice bidding me a final farewell.

"Aeternum vale!"

3

SEVENTEEN

"Go on, don't be frightened," I said to the Chinese doctor. "Don't spare me any fantasy. Today I can listen to everything. No one, alas, will reproach me for that any longer."

"I'm delighted to see you so happy, sir."

"I can see you'll never understand me. Why, I'm overcome with remorse and feel horribly forsaken!"

"I'm so sorry. I had mistaken your condition for jubilation. I've never seen you with such a gleam in your eye. . . . But I'm afraid you may be disappointed in the end of my story, for it's extremely commonplace. In fact, it's merely the inevitable conclusion to the adventure. Perhaps, though, there are a few curious touches to it."

"The touches will console me, I'm sure, venerable sir. Please go on."

"When Chong had come to the end of his statement, the president gave him permission to sit down and a few witnesses were called in. They had no fresh evidence to add. Nothing of any interest."

"What about the woman, Chong's wife?"

"She was also called in—no further interest there, sir, either. She was as she had been described in every detail: skinny, a sluglike complexion, and a sightless face in which no expression could be seen. To crown these advantages, she was more or less incapable of expressing herself coherently. All she lacked was to be dumb!

"The Mandarin President spoke to her severely, reproaching her for not having used her influence over Chong to bring him back to the right path. She did not seem to understand and muttered a few unintelligible words. Then he asked her to confirm her husband's main statements; there he managed to drag a little out of her. Chong had not taken his eyes off this creature from the moment she came in. She, in her turn, after twisting her head around in every direction, seeking his gaze, had set her face toward him. From then on, no further reply could be dragged out of her. In exasperation the Mandarin President dismissed her ignominiously. She disappeared, feeling her way along, and that was the last seen of her."

"I see. In any case, it would have been mad to expect any further enlightenment from her. What happened next?"

"Let me consult my notes. After that . . . here we are: after that the Mandarin President called on the plaintiff to speak."

"The plaintiff? I suppose you mean the attorney general?"

"Not at all, sir. The attorney general represents Society. He will be making his appearance later on. I said the plaintiff—the injured party, if you prefer. Why are you so surprised? Am I not making myself clear? What I mean is, the persons who have suffered damage and are seeking compensation."

"Venerable sir," I quietly said, "this surpasses my wildest hopes. It's difficult to follow you, though. Try to explain yourself more clearly. You never mentioned any plaintiffs before, nor their presence at the tribunal."

"I must have overlooked them, and I apologize for that. It's obvious they attended the tribunal."

"But who were they?"

"Well, first of all, the families of the seven victims, sir. That was the main group. After that—"

"The families of the seven victims! Venerable sir, tell me, tell me at once, in two words, what were their grounds for complaint? You must certainly have jotted down an accurate list of their grievances. I can't be left in ignorance of them a moment longer."

155

"You seem overexcited, sir."

"I beseech you, venerable sir. Each aspect of this trial is more precious to me than a leaf of gold."

"Your haste disturbs my plan. Since you're so impatient, however, I'll tell you that the principal complaint of the families was the 'loss of face' suffered by one of their members."

"Loss of face!"

I gave a start, as though a pin had just been planted in my thigh. For a long minute I looked at him with suspicion.

"Yes, sir," he went on in genuine astonishment. "Isn't that the expression which in your language indicates, however imperfectly, a feeling akin to humiliation, to. . . ."

"Go on," I said, calming down a little. "I'm a ninny. Do you know, for a moment I thought you were joking. I shan't interrupt you again."

"So much the better, sir. Your agitation is incomprehensible to me. It disturbs my train of thought. Well, there were the families of the seven victims. . . . All the members were not there, naturally. Each family had appointed a delegate. Then there were the priests of the three cults, and finally a representative of the clan of executioners.

"The families were by far the most considerable group. It alone included several thousand people, who were, moreover, none too respectable, which was only to be expected. In China every profession is pursued within the framework of the family clan. The profession of bandit is no exception, so that the relatives of those condemned to death were identified with the miscreants of the district."

"Just a moment," I said, turning this over in my mind. "Since you're such a stickler for order, let's recapitulate. Chong had against him, first and foremost, the whole criminal population—isn't that so?"

"That's so."

"And secondly, Society—that's to say the mass of honest citizens who were to voice the main accusation through the mouth of the Mandarin Attorney General, as you told me?"

"Precisely, sir. And in addition, as accessories, the priests and the executioners."

"Go on, venerable sir. I understand now."

"I'm glad to hear it, sir. Here, then, is the representative of the families. The seven delegates, having similar claims, had agreed to have them put forward by one of their number, the oldest and wisest. His claim contained two points: first, he demanded compensation for the damage and grief caused to the families by the death of one of their members. . . ."

"There seems to be a flaw in his wisdom," I observed. "If the words have any meaning, the damage and grief would have been exactly the same without Chong's crime."

"That question gave rise to a lengthy debate. In the end the opinion of the court coincided with yours. In China we all have a strong business sense. We were well aware that the delegate was trying to turn the situation to his advantage, but the judges considered his claim excessive.

"As for the second grievance, it concerned, as I said before, the 'loss of face' inflicted on the members of the clan. This was far more serious. It is quite certain that by preventing the condemned men from carrying out their role in the ceremony and showing a manly attitude, the executioner seemed to have a very low opinion of their courage. The tribunal considered the grievance well-founded, reserving itself the right to fix an appropriate compensation in due course."

"What sort of compensation were the families demanding, then?"

"A substantial sum of money, and the death sentence for Chong. That accounts for the families, sir."

"I see. And the other injured parties?"

"They were admitted, but only with reluctance, so paltry were their grievances compared to the main accusation.

"The executioners' representative felt that the honor of his profession had been besmirched. He claimed a fine as a matter of principle and, needless to say, the death penalty.

"Then it came to the turn of the three priests. They had to assist the condemned men in their final moments on earth, and Chong's intervention had thwarted them. We listened to them in attentive silence, for, even though we are not religiously inclined, we welcome every doctrine and we appreciate symbols. We enjoy hearing a thesis expounded, and their presence promised us some good entertainment."

158

"I'm somewhat Chinese myself on that particular score, venerable sir. What were the theses of the three priests?"

"Quite simple and straightforward. The Buddhist was the first to speak. He explained to us that, in depriving the condemned man of his final quarter of an hour of existence, the executioner no doubt prevented him from performing an act of charity, thereby forcing his soul to be reincarnated in the body of an inferior animal.

"The Taoist priest regarded Chong's initiative as the deprivation of a quarter of an hour which was particularly propitious to mystical emotions and profound meditation. Thus the condemned man lost the best chance in his life of entering into communication with the principle which rules the world.

"Some of the notables took advantage of the situation to ask for a complete explanation on the theory of the transmigration of souls and the precepts of Lao-tzu. We all listened, partly out of curiosity, but above all out of courtesy toward these holy men, who are always somewhat foreign to us and who were in a sense our guests. The crowd was not particularly impressed. We applauded, however, for the sake of politeness, and the bells accompanied this ovation for a decent length of time.

"As for the Confucian sage, he merely said that Chong had violated the ritual. This was a truly Chinese turn of phrase and cheers broke out spontaneously throughout the courtroom.

"After they had explained their doctrines one after

159

the other, they all three came to the conclusion that Chong had failed in every one of them. They therefore agreed to demand a communal compensation—the death sentence.

"These, sir, were the claims of the plaintiffs. The Mandarin Attorney General then took them into consideration, while putting forward his own at the same time. I made a note of his peroration. It's remarkably clear in its conciseness and, moreover, sums up his entire speech. Here it is:

" '. . . In conclusion, notables, Chong's guilt is manifest.

" 'From the strictly juridical point of view Chong had on seven occasions violated the Chinese law that forbids killing. Each of his acts, according to our Code, has a precise qualification. This is not a case of simple homicide. The weapon he used is enough to dispel that illusion. . . . It is the coward's weapon—poison. It is a clear case of intentional murder, a premeditated crime, and punishable by death.

" 'Chong, moreover, has introduced an essentially disturbing element into the traditional order established by our ancestors. This fault, no matter how insignificant, serious enough for an ordinary individual, assumes a sacrilegious character when committed by a mandarin, whose duty precisely is to respect the ritual. For this misdemeanor Chong the executioner is equally liable to the death penalty.

" 'Let us now sum up, notables, the particular circumstances which attended these acts. My task, though painful, is easy, for Chong has accused himself. I shall merely confine myself to drawing your attention to his cynical statements.

" 'He has told you the occasion on which the instinct to kill was born in his brain; but he was incapable of giving a single motive that might explain, if not excuse, this desire. No passion, no fury, blinded him. He bore no particular grudge against the men condemned to death. He therefore acted out of sheer perversity.

" 'He conceived his crimes several years before committing them. Think of that, notables. For more than forty moons he lived with this thought in mind, and during all that time he never had a twinge of shame, not even a reaction of pity for the victims he had chosen and condemned to die with such appalling composure.

" 'To hypocrisy he added evil-mindedness, pretending to repent and submit to the will of his father, whereas he was guided only by the desire to kill.

" 'Finally, notables—you have noticed this, as I have—since appearing before us, Chong has shown no sign of remorse. We were all expecting, you were hoping as I was, for a word of remorse, a gesture, a mere impulse of humanity, which the vilest murderers have at the recollection of the wretches whose existence they have implacably cut short. We were disappointed. Chong the executioner appears, on the contrary, to pride himself on his conduct.

" 'It is therefore my duty, notables, to demand the death sentence for Chong.' "

* *

"I suppose," I said, "that the drums and bells marked the solemnity of this moment as usual?"

"Scarcely, sir. There was no sensation. This conclusion was only to be expected, and our curiosity was distracted by the approach of the next development —the advocate's plea."

"I'm in the same frame of mind, venerable sir, I must admit. I carry my love of paradox to such lengths that I am swooning to hear the arguments put forward by the advocate in defense of such an untenable cause."

E I G H T E E N

"This advocate was a knowledgeable sage himself, sir, reputed for his wisdom, his subtlety, and also for his talent for discovering arguments that had occurred to no one else. He did not disappoint us. I also think he'll satisfy your desire, which I think I discern, to witness a brilliant mind and more than average learning put to the service of the most execrable iniquity.

"Here is the advocate. He collects his thoughts. He greets the mandarins and the notables ceremoniously. He begins as follows:

" 'Notables, I wish first of all to take a purely juridical position. I am going to permit myself in all humility to contradict certain conclusions of the illustrious Mandarin Attorney General. He has presented Chong's case as a clear one. And so it is in fact, but I shall show you that its clarity is not what he fancied it to be.

" 'For this, it is necessary for me to read you a few documents, which no one has so far mentioned in this case despite their importance. You know them well. I merely wish to recall them to your memory and ask you to weigh each phrase in them when you come to decide on my client's fate.'

"At this stage, sir, he paused for a moment, while the court sat silent, intrigued by this opening and impressed by his composure. Eventually he drew several scrolls from his wide sleeves, unrolled one of them, and began reading:

" 'Judgment of the High Court of Yi-Ping, dated the. . . . Whereas. . . . '—I'll leave out the unimportant details—'The Court, with the concurrence of the notables, declares the accused Lee guilty of murder, denies him the benefit of extenuating circumstances, and *sentences him to death.* . . .

" 'This,' the advocate remarked, 'is the sentence passed by the tribunal as the conclusion to the case of the accused man Lee. Lee, I would remind you, notables, was the first condemned man to be executed by Chong: the object of his first crime according to the prosecution's contention . . . *the sentence passed by this court,* I repeat, Mandarin President. This official document is signed by Your Honor. It is

164

likewise initialed by you, notables, and witnessed by the illustrious Mandarin Attorney General.'

"At that moment, sir, I noticed, a barely perceptible murmur betrayed the pleasure which began to grip the public, and their hope. The Chinese man in the street, who is sharp-witted, realized that this reading of the document and this insistence on dotting the i's and crossing the t's augured some special entertainment. He discerned some surprising development, without knowing exactly what the advocate was leading up to. Mystery added to his pleasure."

"I think I can discern it fairly clearly myself," I said.

"I congratulate you . . . but don't spoil my pleasure, for I'm reliving this scene with passion.

"The advocate methodically put his scroll away, unrolled another, and started reading again:

" 'Judgment of the High Court of Yi-Ping, dated the. . . . Whereas. . . . The Court, with the concurrence of the notables, declares the accused Sao guilty of murder, denies him the benefit of extenuating circumstances, and *sentences him to death*. . . .

" ' "Sentences him to death," notables,' he repeated. 'This term has a remarkably precise meaning that cannot be disputed and to which I would ask Your Graces to give the closest attention. Sao, I must remind you, by the way, is the second victim whom the prosecution attributes to my client, the executioner Chong.' "

"I had guessed as much, venerable sir," I said.

"We all had some notion of it, sir. But we were grateful to the advocate for taking this line, for letting his intentions sink in gradually, of their own accord, by infusing them with a grisly atmosphere of uncertainty. The murmur of the crowd that now accompanied each of his gestures became slightly more pronounced when he was seen to unroll yet another scroll and prepare to read it out loud."

"I wager it was to do with the third man condemned to death."

"Yes, sir."

"And the sentence was identical?"

"The sentence was identical, word for word."

"In that case, venerable sir, it's superfluous to read it out again. I, too, am breathless with curiosity, and we're wasting time. Let's proceed to the seventh judgment."

"Sir, I am pained to witness such impatience. In China we like to savor our pleasures slowly."

"I can understand that, but you yourself are destroying the effect of surprise. Go on, I beseech you."

"So be it, since you disdain refinements. I shall go straight on to the seventh sentence.

" 'The Court, with the concurrence of the notables, declares the accused Yuan guilty of murder, denies him the benefit of extenuating circumstances, and *sentences him to death.*'

"The advocate paused once more. He waited, in an attitude of the most profound meditation, for these seven successive readings to take their effect. Then he went on:

" 'This is recorded by brush, in black on white, with legally prescribed ink and in the form laid down by the ritual. This is approved and signed by every one of you. May I now be allowed in all humility to put a question to the members of this tribunal? I ask you, notables, I ask you, learned Mandarin President, I ask you, illustrious Mandarin Attorney General, if any of you contests the authenticity or validity of these documents?'

" 'No,' replied the mandarins. 'No,' replied the notables. 'No,' replied the Mandarin Attorney General. 'These documents, we guarantee, are perfectly authentic and valid.'

" 'May I further ask if, among the same members of this august Court, there is anyone who feels today in his just man's mind that these sentences are illegal or contrary to equity?'

" 'No,' replied all the officials with one voice, and with still greater insistence. 'No, certainly not. These are good, just, and equitable sentences.'

" 'I note your sage reply,' the wily advocate went on in a rather more solemn tone, 'and I thank you for it.

" 'Now, this is the honorable Mandarin Attorney General's point which I take leave to contradict. He has said: Chong bears full responsibility for his crimes. The urge to kill was in him. He premeditated his offenses on his own. . . . Is it not, on the contrary, clear to you in the first place that this desire, this intention to kill, should be ascribed to the signatories of these sentences and, secondly, that this

167

desire and intention conform to the law both in spirit and to the letter—this law that, according to the prosecution, has been violated?'

"Scarcely had he finished speaking, sir, when the drums and bells broke out at full pitch, indicating the emotion and almost sensual overexcitement of the assembly."

"You were quite right, venerable sir," I observed. "If the conclusion of your story is simple, its finer shades, as you led me to expect, are full of curiosity. This advocate fascinates me. Don't stop. What did he say next?"

"Nothing, sir, for quite a long time; for the drums went on rolling, the bells ringing, and a brisk agitation reigned in the courtroom. The magistrates whispered in one another's ears. The president exchanged irritable signs with the attorney general. The advocate stood motionless, his head bowed, his arms folded across his chest, his hands concealed in the sleeves of his robe, in an attitude of extreme deference.

"It was the Mandarin Attorney General who first spoke as soon as order was re-established. He was visibly overwrought, which diminished his prestige in the eyes of the crowd. He did not seem to be in possession of his usual self-control. He declared:

" 'The eminent advocate, notables, is trying to sow confusion in your minds in an underhand manner. Do not allow yourselves to be swayed by his dialectic. The case is clear, I repeat, and all his efforts are merely designed to obscure it. The law of the province of Li-Kang is specific and allows for no exceptions. No one has the right to make an attempt on the life of his fellow man. Chong has killed. Chong has admitted acting with premeditation. Chong has committed seven murders. The blood of his seven victims cries out for revenge.'

"The advocate then turned around slightly and, with his usual composure, addressed himself to him directly:

" 'I see I have not succeeded in convincing my honorable contradictor. Am I to understand that, in his eyes, the seven condemned men are *victims?*'

" 'Precisely,' the Mandarin Attorney General stoutly declared. 'Victims.'

"At this point, sir, the Mandarin President opened his mouth as though he were about to speak. He cast a furious glance at the Mandarin Attorney General, but the latter in his excitement failed to notice.

" 'I crave his indulgence for my insistence,' the advocate went on, without allowing his rival to say a word, 'but I must ask him to be even more specific. Does he consider that the individuals Lee, Sao, Yuan, and the others were killed contrary to our sacred rites? Does he assert that the act which cut short their lives is a culpable, inhuman act and must be punished by law—that is, literally, murder?'

" 'Without a shadow of doubt,' the Mandarin Attorney General heatedly exclaimed, adding, 'Life is a gift from heaven. . . .'

" 'I take note of that, Mandarin President,' the advocate broke in, raising his head again. 'I see that the illustrious Mandarin Attorney General is fiercely opposed to the death sentence. The sentences passed by this tribunal, which I had the honor to read out to you, he considers illegal, inhuman and criminal.'

"At this the Mandarin Attorney General flushed, sir, and tears came into his eyes as he protested violently, even forgetting the rules of politeness.

" 'Not at all!' he shouted, clutching the rail in front of him with his clenched fists. 'The advocate, Mandarin President, is trying to lend a perfidious sense to my words. I never meant that. It is beyond all doubt, it is only too obvious, that Society as represented by this tribunal has the right and duty to condemn guilty men to death. But this is the case of an individual . . . an *individual,* notables, that's my point and I would ask you to bear it in mind. I maintain that no individual has the right to act as an instrument of Justice.'

" 'Not even a mandarin in the service of Justice?' the advocate inquired, raising his voice slightly.

" 'Certainly not!' the Mandarin Attorney General stormed. 'He, least of all. A mandarin is paid to administer the law, not violate it.'

" 'Not even the executioner?'

" 'Look out, it's a trap!' I in my turn shouted, caught up in the turmoil of this debate.

" 'Be quiet, sir—!'

" 'Not even the execu—!' the Mandarin Attorney General burst out.

"He stopped in mid-sentence, I noticed. He went scarlet in the face, a deeper red than his ceremonial robe. The fantastic convulsions of the embroidered dragon on his breast betrayed the palpitations of his heart. His hands trembled. Beads of sweat broke out on his forehead, turning the colors of his make-up into a grayish paste. His false beard seemed to bristle under the effect of his indignation. His skullcap was askew. His pigtail hung down, lamentable and inert, like a grotesque and obscene symbol revealing, for all to see, that he was about to lose face shamefully.

"The two rivals stood facing each other amid the tumult of the drums and cymbals, accompanied by the shrieks and stamping of the crowd. The spectacle, sir, was rare to behold. The Mandarin Attorney General, it must be admitted, was not in a strong position. The craftiness of the defense had put him in a state of rage unusual for a Chinese dignitary and that made him ridiculous in the eyes of the people. He had fallen like a child into the trap you discerned. The advocate, it is true, had shown diabolical cunning and conducted the debate with the manifest intention of putting him out of countenance. He had prepared this new effect with extraordinary talent, speaking first of all in a very quiet, almost humble tone, then gradually raising his voice and thundering out his last retort: 'Not even the executioner!' with a flutter of sleeves which caused an intoxicating draft. He had unquestionably humiliated his contradictor, and the Chinese showed their enthusiasm with loud cheers. Chong's cause had gained ground in the mind of the crowd, but the mandarin magistrates and the notables looked uneasy and irritated.

"This is how the advocate continued his attack, sir, as soon as the storm had abated a little:

" 'Not even, great mandarins, when the executioner acts on an order signed by you, like an obedient little mandarin? Not even when he carries out *to the letter* the prescriptions of these other documents I shall now read out to you and which are likewise signed by you? Here, for example: the condemned man Lee, the condemned man Sao—there are seven of them, notables, the seven alleged victims of my client—the condemned man Yuan will be handed over to the executioner. He will take charge of him and *proceed with his execution.*

" ' "And proceed with his execution"—that, too, is written down in black on white, Mandarin President. The words of the Chinese language have one meaning only. Far be it from me to try and obscure this debate, as my honorable contradictor has accused me of doing. On the contrary, I wish to restore it to the schematic simplicity which his wisdom refuses to perceive, because it wanders off on points of detail. I shall lay the question bare before you and you will see it revealed in all its stark purity.

" "To sum up the juridical aspect of this case: concerning these so-called victims, there was a sentence passed by you, an unassailable and utterly equitable sentence, condemning them to death. There was subsequently an order, likewise given by you to the executioner Chong, an order his duty *forbade* him to shirk—the order to execute those condemned to death. Chong, as a mandarin respectful of the law, took charge of these condemned men and took their life. Chong executed them. He was an obedient, irresponsible, and innocent instrument. He acted legally and cannot incur any punishment.'

"That, sir, was the argument put forward by the advocate from the strictly juridical point of view."

NINETEEN

"There's a really able advocate," I remarked.

"Yes, indeed. He was extremely clever—a little too clever even, and in the end he failed to win his case."

"You don't seem to appreciate his arguments?"

"They are what is known, I believe, in your language as sophistry; to my mortification, you referred to them as *chinoiseries*. I admit that many Chinese are partial to them—the applause of the assembly showed this only too clearly. But that sort of reasoning, attractive enough at first glance, always has a point of extreme weakness that neither art nor eloquence can conceal indefinitely. The whole edifice collapses as soon as one puts one's finger on this point.

"The president adjourned the hearing—a wise measure that allowed the Mandarin Attorney General to recover his composure and think things out. On resuming, he had no difficulty in refuting the advocate's thesis, as you shall now see."

"I beseech you, venerable sir, first of all satisfy my curiosity. What was the accused doing all this time? You haven't mentioned him again. What was his attitude during this verbal tussle?"

"Incomprehensible, sir. He didn't intervene at any stage. His face expressed complete indifference. He was apparently the only one to take no interest in this battle of wits. His gaze was once more fixed on the ceiling, so much so that the Mandarin President, who was slightly vexed by the advocate's maneuvers, called him to order and dryly enjoined him to show a little more respect. All to no purpose—he maintained this detachment right up to the very end.

"After the adjournment, then, the Mandarin President, who had turned the matter over in his mind and readjusted his robe, had no difficulty in destroying the specious argument. He begged leave to speak and said:

" 'Notables, the plea of the eminent advocate is brilliant, but it is only a plea. He is confusing—intentionally, I'm sure, for he is too skilled to do so by mistake—two acts which have nothing to do with each other.

" 'Acting on the orders of the tribunal, and according to the ritual laid down by the law, the executioner fulfills a legal function, whereas the individual Chong, by anticipating the executioner's gesture contrary to this ritual, commits a murder. That is the whole crux of the matter. Chong cannot be regarded as the instrument of Justice since he did not make use of the proper instrument: the sword. Your sentences did not prescribe poisoning and therefore cannot excuse him. This is quite clear to all of you, and it is useless for me to offer further proof. I shall merely quote an example of a striking analogy: a soldier who brings down his foe in wartime acts legitimately, whereas he is a murderer if he kills the same individual before the declaration of hostilities.'

"This was the voice of reason. The assembly showed that they were satisfied by giving a long-drawn murmur. The advocate's intervention had entertained them for a moment, but the wise Chinese people, though they enjoy being carried away for a short while by the attraction of intellectual fantasy, know how to pull themselves together in time and come down to earth again very quickly. The advocate realized he would never be able to topple this massive battlement of common sense. From then on he appeared spiritless. He had emitted all his sparks in one fell swoop, like those fireworks whose fuses go off simultaneously. The Chinese accord them a passing acknowledgment, but they show their real esteem for a better maintained household.

"But, realizing now that he had won the day, sir,

the Mandarin Attorney General in his turn gave evidence of diabolical ingenuity. Listen to this final, terrible shaft he hurls at his opponent:

"'Not only, notables, did Chong not obey your orders, but he surreptitiously *prevented* the execution of your sentences. Through his fault the condemned men Lee, Sao, Yuan, and the others *did not undergo* the punishment you saw proper to inflict on them. They therefore did not atone for their crime, and Justice was thwarted yet again. I would ask the tribunal to bear in mind this additional crime which I had omitted and that the plea of the eminent advocate suggested to me.'"

"Enough," I begged. "I beseech you, venerable sir. No Westerner can hold out for long against such an orgy of ingenuity, not even I. I ask for mercy. My head's in a whirl."

"It's all over, sir. But, for the Attorney General to have his revenge, it was necessary for the advocate to lose face in his turn. This is what happened, and the public applauded his defeat as warmly as it had celebrated his victory.

"Honor was saved. The game had ended in a draw. All the mandarins heaved a sigh of relief; then, out of politeness, they gave their attention to the two opponents' respective points of view. They analyzed them, they dissected them, and there was a general discussion during which all the articles of our Code were brought up. I shall spare you all this, for it can't interest anyone but a specialist. In conclusion, as was only to be expected, the Court decided in favor of the Mandarin Attorney General, but mitigated the humiliation of the advocate by rendering homage to his ability and talent.

"Foiled on the juridical plane, he then pleaded insanity, as I told you. It was the only possible defense. If Chong's attitude had not made such an unfavorable impression on the notables, he might have had a chance of winning them over, for it was a fine speech he gave."

"The advocate also believed his client to be insane," I muttered.

"At all events he pretended to think so, and his tone was sincere. Listen to this, for instance:

" 'Are you fully aware, notables, of the acts that have brought my client here? The murder of some wretches already condemned to death and with no more than a quarter of an hour to live? No one can seriously maintain that this is the behavior of an individual of sound mind. The Mandarin Attorney General has declared that Chong could not possibly have had any grudge against his victims. I, for my part, would add that he had no *interest* in doing away with them. He had nothing to gain from their death. The only conclusion is that he is insane. There's not a shadow of a motive for his crimes."

"Still this question of motive," I said.

"Still the same question, sir. The advocate did his duty and tried to exploit this mystery to the full. He showed that Chong's insanity dated back several years; that it was provoked by the emotion of his attempted suicide, by the death of the dog, and by an inexplicable dream. According to him, Chong had been living ever since in a state of hallucination. As proof, he put forward that senseless journey of his and his morbid attachment to that bottle. To cut a long story short, he did his utmost to turn the most unfavorable of his client's statements to his advantage.

"But, as the Mandarin Attorney General pointed out to him once more, absence of motive did not necessarily argue insanity. On the contrary, taken in conjunction with such logical reasoning as Chong's, with a will power as strong as his, and a persistently evil intent that overcame all obstacles, it could only perhaps be attributed to one state of mind—perversity."

TWENTY

"It was this word *perversity,* sir, that put the finishing touch to the case. It was to this that all the hypotheses that could be erected in this affair led back.

"I shall now come to the conclusion—which you have already guessed, I am sure."

"You can be quite sure," I muttered resentfully. "Don't worry, Satan, I recognized you long ago. I've let you have your say, but you haven't deceived me. I smelled the fire and brimstone as soon as you appeared. Finish your job. Tell me the conclusion. I'm sure it will fulfill all my hopes and reinforce my optimism as to human destiny."

"Your language, sir, is incomprehensible, but I shall do as you wish.

"Chong the executioner was condemned to death. No other sentence could have been given. The entire population of Li-Kang cried out for his head, even the lowest strata of the population, who would not forgive him for having chosen poor destitute wretches as his victims. The corps of notables was unanimous. Thus the case came to an end.

"But I should like to come back just once more, sir, to the mysterious question of motive. It prevents me from sleeping at night, I must confess, and I cannot resign myself to classifying it among the insoluble problems."

The old Chinese had assumed an attitude of profound meditation. His eyes reflected the dark infinity of abysmal spiritual depths. I admired him in spite of myself. He made me think inevitably of Rodin's *Thinker*. He appeared to me as the personification of human genius in its painful and eternal struggle toward greater lucidity, toward a more and more intimate communion with the glorious secrets of the universe.

"Everything has been said, sir, on the subject of these extraordinary crimes. Everything was said, I know, at the hearing and at the sages' discussions. The infamy of that fellow Chong surpasses the limits of one's imagination, I grant you. But none the less, the fact remains, he was a *man*. I examined him several times, as a doctor, and with passionate interest, as you may well imagine. He was normal from the psychological point of view. He showed no pathological strain, and several of my colleagues in psychiatry assured me of the integrity of his mental faculties. He was, as I said before, a human being, constituted and organized to all outward appearances like every other Chinese person—like you and me, sir."

"Like you and me, venerable sir," I pondered.

"And as long as I live I shall maintain that a being of that sort must always obey a motive, no matter how fantastic it may be. There is a cause for every one of his acts. That is the essential difference between our voluntary movements and the reflexes of wild beasts. Don't you agree?"

"Between us and wild beasts . . . I agree with you entirely, venerable sir."

"Well, sir, in spite of all the efforts of the tribunal, the mystery remained unsolved.

"Each time he was referred to this subject, Chong harked back again and again to his hallucination. He digressed on his so-called mission. But on the *why* of his frenzy, he still shed no light at all. Toward the end of the final hearing the Mandarin President advised him several times, in his own interests, to make a complete confession on this point, as he had on all the others. The notables made the same request. The advocate, when he saw the case was lost, sided with them, for he knew that his client's refusal would entail a more severe sentence than the simple death penalty. We Chinese do not like the irrational, and the less we understand something the more severely do we punish it.

"All their efforts were wasted, sir. Every now and then, however, Chong seemed to make a genuine effort to explain himself, as though he were trying to interpret a difficult truth, but it never came to anything."

The expression on the face of the old Chinese underwent a further change. His tone became almost solemn as he tried to extract the philosophical essence of his story. No doubt this was a further ruse of his. He belonged to a race that beats drums and rings bells to mark the emotional stages of existence. But the artifice of his attitude aped the signs of genuine emotion so closely as to be taken for them.

"He took his secret with him to the tomb, sir. No one will ever decipher it now. Maybe he was sincere, after all, when he appeared to struggle as he did with an inexplicable mystery. Maybe he was not sufficiently educated, not sufficiently knowledgeable, to grasp the real reasons for his behavior. Maybe, too, his silence was the will of heaven. Maybe those reasons were of too atrocious a nature to be uttered aloud. Maybe the universal order forbade the scandal of a revelation that might have inspired weak minds with unwholesome ideas."

"Maybe . . . maybe he didn't want to blow his own trumpet," I said.

The old man looked at me with an expression of alarm.

"Sir, you sometimes make remarks that baffle me, but I can't help wondering whether you're not a bit of a cynic."

"Don't bother about me, venerable sir. I don't exist . . . I thank you for your story. It's simple and strange, as you promised. But one of your last statements surprises me, I must admit. You said something about a punishment more severe than the simple death penalty. Does this mean you've got another subject of wonder hidden up your sleeve?"

Slowly he stretched out his hand and seized his chopsticks he had laid down beside him. He began manipulating them with a dexterity that could only be described as prodigious. I was reminded of a gigantic crustacean armed with delicate pincers.

"That's correct, sir," he said. "But I don't know if I ought. . . ."

"Finish your job," I cried. "Let's have it all. I want to drain the cup to the dregs!"

"If you insist. . . . This is it:

"Just think, sir. Everyone was too indignant to be satisfied with a simple decapitation. Public opinion cried out for exemplary punishment. Furthermore, the plaintiffs had not been able to obtain the financial compensation to which they were entitled. Chong was a poor man. They had to be given compensation. In matters of repression, as in all other matters, it's the finer shades that distinguish civilized nations. The high mandarins therefore decided to inflict one of our Old World punishments on Chong.

184

"It is, I believe, a punishment peculiar to China—a rather slow one. We have recourse to this only in the most serious cases. Our ancestors, who invented it, succeeded in endowing it with a character at once shameful and painful, thereby adding humiliation to mental agony.

"Chong expiated his crimes, sir. I give you my word, the punishment was in proportion to the offense. I don't see any point in describing this scene to you, but if you like. . . ."

"Satan!" I yelled. "I recognized you, I tell you. You would be quite capable of treating me to all the refinements of Chinese torture, just to crown your impertinent story! I don't want to hear about the tortures at any price. Stop waving your chopsticks about like pincers. Take your claws out of my heart! I've no more curiosity. I'm satisfied with your accursed tale . . . I'm certain, after having heard it, that the punishment was in proportion to the crime!"

"Have no doubt on that score, sir. I can vouch for it better than anyone else, since I witnessed it."

"You witnessed it!"

"From start to finish, as a medical expert. The tribunal had renewed its confidence in me, in fact, after sentencing me to a small fine. I did my best to acquit myself worthily and was careful to avoid all negligence. Although it was extremely long, I assure you I did not let my attention stray for a single second.

"You may be sure, too, that this time no one disturbed the order of the ceremony. As you can well imagine, the precedent of Chong was a salutary warning and the new executioner was closely supervised. Extraordinary precautions had been taken to avoid any untimely intervention. Chong remained fully conscious right up to the moment ordained by the ritual."

The old Chinese pulled himself together and, as I mopped my brow, finally added:

"Moreover, in my opinion, sir, these precautions were superfluous. Creatures like that fellow Chong are exceptional and few and far between. They are not common phenomena, lucky for us. According to Chinese statistics, they only appear at the rate of one every two or three thousand years. And they commit crimes that are so monstrous, so contrary to every human instinct, that they never encourage disciples."